QUICKSAND POND

JANET TAYLOR LISLE

Atheneum Books for Young Readers

New York   London   Toronto   Sydney   New Delhi

ATHENEUM BOOKS FOR YOUNG READERS

An imprint of Simon & Schuster Children's Publishing Division

1230 Avenue of the Americas, New York, New York 10020

ATHENEUM BOOKS FOR YOUNG READERS

is a registered trademark of Simon & Schuster, Inc.

Atheneum logo is a trademark of Simon & Schuster, Inc.

For information about special discounts for bulk purchases, please contact Simon & Schuster Special Sales at 1-866-506-1949 or business@simonandschuster.com.

The Simon & Schuster Speakers Bureau can bring authors to your live event. For more information or to book an event, contact the Simon & Schuster Speakers Bureau at 1-866-248-3049 or visit our website at www.simonspeakers.com.

Book design by Tom Daly

The text for this book was set in Adobe Garamond.

Manufactured in the United States of America

0417 FFG

First Edition

2 4 6 8 10 9 7 5 3 1

Library of Congress Cataloging-in-Publication Data

Names: Lisle, Janet Taylor, author.

Title: Quicksand Pond / Janet Taylor Lisle.

Description: First edition. | New York : Atheneum Books for Young Readers, [2017] | Summary: Twelve-year-old Jessie spends the summer with her family on Quicksand Pond, a New England vacation spot, where she develops a star-crossed friendship with independent Terri, and meets a reclusive old lady whose connection to a murder that took place decades ago still informs her present—and affects Terri in ways that Jessie gradually comes to understand the more time they spend together. Identifiers: LCCN 2016009707 ISBN 978-1-4814-7222-7 (hardcover) | ISBN 978-1-4814-7224-1 (eBook) Subjects: | CYAC: Ponds—Fiction. | Friendship—Fiction. | Murder—Fiction. Classification: LCC PZ7.L6912 Qu 2017 | DDC [Fic]—dc23 LC record available at https://lccn.loc.gov/2016009707

FOR JOPLIN AND TIMONY

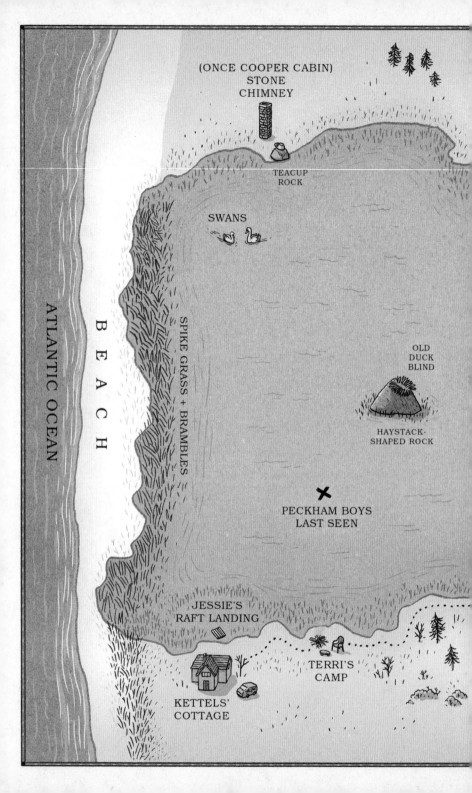

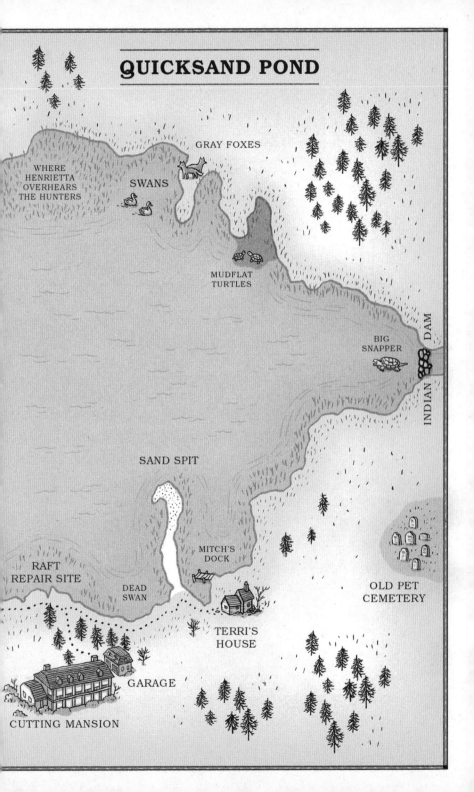

Could I but ride indefinite,
    As doth the meadow-bee,
And visit only where I liked,
    And no man visit me,

And flirt all day with buttercups,
    And marry whom I may,
And dwell a little everywhere,
    Or better, run away

With no police to follow,
    Or chase me if I do,
Till I should jump peninsulas
    To get away from you,—

I said, but just to be a bee
    Upon a raft of air,
And row in nowhere all day long,
    And anchor off the bar,—
What liberty! So captives deem
    Who tight in dungeons are.

                    —Emily Dickinson

QUICKSAND
POND

The two boys who vanished in the pond that night were farm kids, cousins of some kind. They had the same last name, Peckham. Terri Carr told the story to Jessie the day they met on the raft.

"It was summer, just like now," Terri said. "They boasted they could swim across this pond. They waded in before anyone could stop them. They were showing off for their friends."

"Well, what happened?" Jessie asked.

"They disappeared."

"So they drowned?"

"Sucked down is what people say."

"No one tried to rescue them?"

"No one saw where they went. Their bodies were never found."

Jessie said that was impossible. She said the friends on shore would've heard the boys cry out. Someone would've gone for help. The parents of the boys would've had the pond searched, dragged the bottom, if necessary.

"People don't allow other people to just disappear."

"Since when?"

"Since, I don't know, always."

Terri smiled, exposing a darkish row of crooked teeth that could have used a visit to the dentist.

"Look, the main thing is those boys never did turn up. I thought you might like to know. You're the one who's been out here all week on this old pile of lumber."

She meant the raft, the one they were both standing on in the middle of the pond, up to their ankles in water.

"You've been watching me?"

Terri smiled again. "Oh, I knew we'd meet up sometime," she said.

The pond was called Quicksand Pond. It was a long expanse of freshwater that lay just inland from the ocean shore. Back in the days of farms, whole cows had disappeared there. Terri said she knew this because she was born on the pond. Her family had lived there for 150 years.

She explained how a cow, wading in at the edge, would step out too far and sink into a soft pit of mud. Quicksand, it was called. The cow would bellow and thrash, but that only made things worse. Slowly, horribly, the poor beast went down out of sight. The next day the farmer would have to come with a team of horses and pull the carcass out. But just as with the Peckham boys, he wouldn't always find it.

"I've seen skeletons," Terri said. "Down there, under the water."

Even if they were true, these were old stories, or Jessie

assumed they were old, because the pond looked too shallow for anyone to drown in now. Its banks were too clogged with vegetation to seem dangerous. You couldn't even see it from the road because a scrub forest had crept in around it, obscuring at every turn the bright eye of water that lay within. It was invisible from the beach because of the barrier dunes that protected it, dunes grown thick with spike-grass and brambles.

"Most people don't know that anything is even back here," Jessie would say later, after she and Terri had become friends and were spending their days together on the raft. By "people" she meant the well-to-do families who summered nearby in second homes, or the weekend vacationers who came to the beach.

Terri, who never went to the beach and did not even own a bathing suit, said, "So don't tell them, okay? It's just between you and me."

"Don't worry," Jessie had assured her. "The less of them the better, as far as I'm concerned."

No one needed a hidden, half-forgotten pond more than Jessie that summer, and right from the beginning—their first day on the raft—Terri Carr seemed the perfect person to show it to her.

"See that house? A murder happened there." Terri pointed across the water to where a vast and elegant roof rose up through the bushes on shore. She said years ago some men had gone in at night and killed the owners, a husband and wife.

"They shot them dead while their little girl was sleeping upstairs."

Jessie was shocked. "How terrible!"

"She still lives here."

"Who?"

"The girl. In that same house. She's an old woman now."

"Did they catch who did it?"

Terri paused. She looked across the pond to where a family of swans was just coasting in for a landing. Not until every bird was safely down did she turn back to Jessie.

"They caught someone. There was a trial. He got life in prison."

"Well, good."

"But it was a mistake. That person didn't shoot them. He wasn't even there. It was somebody else, except no one could ever prove it, so the innocent man spent forty years in the Lewisburg Penitentiary. He died there."

"How do you know? How do you know he didn't do it?" Jessie asked.

"Because I know," Terri Carr said. "I know everything that happened around here. I see everything that's happening now. I watched you and your family move in last week. I saw all the stuff you brought with you."

ONE

There was always a lot of stuff when the Kettels traveled. They arrived that July in a car crammed with duffels and backpacks, beach towels and lawn chairs, fishing poles and board games, an outdoor grill, an espresso machine, two laptops, three smartphones, and a pair of high-powered binoculars for watching birdlife.

Their cottage, which was rented, looked sadly unprepared for this wealth of possessions.

"I see a clothesline out back," Jessie's father said in the silence after the motor shut down. "Therein lies hidden meaning."

"What meaning?" asked Jonathan from the rear seat.

Richard Kettel raised his black-rimmed glasses and massaged the tender sides of his nose. "The gods of good housekeeping are angry with us. Our summer palace is not equipped with a dryer."

"Ha, ha," said Jonathan. "There are no gods of good housekeeping. Dad made that up, right?" He turned to Jessie beside him, but she looked away.

Their father shook his head. "The washing machine is a relic from the Dark Ages."

"How do you know?" asked Jonathan.

"I hear voices wailing from the Great Beyond."

"I hear birds," Jonathan said, and they all sat still while a flock of bleating seagulls flapped by overhead.

"Looks like the roof is kind of falling off," Julia observed from the front seat, which she'd occupied, as if by divine right, the whole way from Pittsburgh. "There are chunks of wood all over the lawn."

"Lawn? Is that what that is?"

"It used to be one," Jonathan said. "It grew up, that's all."

"It grew up. Now I see." Their father took off his glasses and squinted. "There's probably no dishwasher, either. What is that thing on the front step?"

Everyone leaned forward. Something with a long neck was sitting outside the door.

"A toilet plunger?" Julia ventured. "That's what it looks like. And a bucket, I think, off to the side."

"I hoped I was going blind," said their father, a high school English teacher with a taste for gallows humor. "I hoped I'd gone mad and was having hallucinations."

"No," Julia said, "it's a plunger. Does that mean . . ."

"Fraud and deceit!" Richard Kettel yanked open the car door. He stepped out unsteadily, as if the ground were the deck of an oceangoing vessel. Well, they were near the sea, Jessie thought. Quite near, though not actually on it. "Rhode Island saltbox," the listing had read. "Short walk to the beach. Three bedrooms, two baths, bed linens supplied." They'd rented, sight unseen, for six weeks till the middle of August.

"I see something else!" Jonathan shouted. "Look, over there! I see a dragonfly, or it could be a moth, and now I'm looking at a whole mess of other things. See by the fence? Bugs!"

"Excellent," said their father from outside the car. "Just what we need."

At that moment Jessie bolted. She was out of the car in one jump, running away across the overgrown lawn. It wasn't only that she needed to get away, immediately, though that was certainly true. She'd spied something, a flicker of silvery water coming through tall reeds at the lawn's far end. She pushed her way through and arrived on a shore. Not the sandy ocean beach she'd expected, but the mud shore of a pond whose waters spread away from her, smooth and blue in the sun.

Cattails grew high all around the edges. Off to her right the pond slipped around a bend, as if more was there to be discovered. Across the way a single snow-white swan fed along a shadowed bank. Jessie let out her breath and for one perfect moment she felt happy. She felt like a swan herself, one that had just flown in from a perilous journey.

She was in a separatist mood that year, her twelfth, and in a state of irritation with everyone around her. She was irritated with her father because he looked at her with skeptical eyes and said things like "May I ask how you came to that conclusion?"

She was at odds with her older sister, Julia, because Julia was so pathetically nice to everyone. Whoever they were, whatever they said, Julia smiled and agreed.

"What is wrong with you?" Jessie demanded. "You didn't use to be this way."

"What way?" Julia asked.

"I don't know. So spineless."

"You shouldn't say things like that. It just makes you look ignorant," Julia replied.

The problem with Jessie's mother was that she worked night and day at her office in Pittsburgh. And that summer, thanks to their father dragging them off to practically the end of the earth (as Jessie had declared this New England beach town to be), she wouldn't possibly find time to visit.

"This is not the end of the earth," Jonathan had said.

"I just meant—"

"There can't be an end to the earth because the earth is round."

"I *know* it's round!"

"So why did you say . . ."

The trouble with her brother, Jonathan, was that he was six years old.

Jessie watched a second swan arrive to join the first across the pond. Hardly had it landed when a crunch of feet sounded behind her. A body crashed through the reeds. Julia. In all her splendor. Everyone stared at her wherever she went.

"It's only a pond," Julia said, coming up to stand beside her sister. "Where's the sea?"

Jessie pointed. "I think the beach must be down there."

Julia shaded her eyes. "Looks like miles away. Dad

said it would be closer. He should've let Mom make the arrangements. He never gets things right."

Julia was beautiful, everyone said so. She had a heart-shaped face, unblemished skin, and chocolate-brown eyes with thick black lashes that curled up naturally at the ends. She would never in her life need a drop of mascara. A perfect stranger had stopped her on the sidewalk and asked, "Are you a model? . . . No? Well, you should be, my dear."

"Maybe it's shorter by the road," Jessie told her. "The real estate agents said we could walk to it."

"I think I'll drive," Julia said, which was not a boast. She was sixteen and had her license.

Julia didn't boast about herself. She'd become too polite. She'd thanked the perfect stranger for his compliment. She seemed oblivious to the boys who wolf-whistled on the street. When her computer literacy teacher, Mr. Clarke, invited her to go with him—as a student representative, he said—to a poetry reading upstate, Julia said it was because he admired her poems.

"Are you going to let her go?" Jessie had asked their mother.

"No."

"She'll be mad."

"I'm sure."

"She thinks she's a poet," Jessie said. "A serious poet."

Her mother looked amused. "Julia's new in her skin, so she's trying things out. She doesn't fully understand her effect on people."

"Oh, don't worry, she understands," Jessie had informed her. "She understands perfectly well. She just pretends not to."

Now, standing beside her sister, Jessie felt the pond, too, begin to fall under Julia's power. Its private gaze shifted from Jessie—short, with thick legs and brown, rabbity hair—to Julia, tall and dark and carelessly perfect.

Jessie picked up a large rock and heaved it into the water. Julia backed up and shrieked. "Why did you do that? I'm drenched! You are so impossible!" She huffed off toward the house.

The pond also seemed to retreat after this. The sun went behind a cloud. The swans rose off the water and flew away. The reeds took on a mean look around the water's edge and, removing their magical protection of a minute ago, allowed the sound of voices to come through.

"Just as I predicted, there's no clothes dryer in this house," Jessie heard her father say. "And of course no dishwasher."

"There's a washing machine, though," Jonathan's voice piped up cheerfully. "You said there wouldn't be, and there is, I saw it."

"What I said was, the washing machine would be from the Dark Ages. But I was wrong."

"You were?"

"It's from the French Revolution."

"What's the French Revolution?"

"A time of torture and beheadings. A time of madness and despair. A time of . . ."

Jessie stopped listening. Something was floating in the

water off to her right. It was a wood platform of some kind. She saw rusted nails and a board's sawed-off edge. She bent and reached to draw it closer, but the platform bobbed away.

Behind her a car door slammed and the voices of her family broke through again.

Julia: "I can't get a signal on my cell phone."

Jonathan: "Let me see."

"Look. It's not working."

"I see one bar. Nope, now it's gone."

"Dad! There's no reception here."

"Well, call the police."

"Dad! What are we supposed to do? We're cut off."

"I saw something that looked like a telephone pole on the way in, with wires attached."

"But what about my laptop? It won't work either! No way there's Wi-Fi here."

"Such is life."

"What do you mean, 'such is life'? It might be your life, but it's not mine. I need to be in touch," Julia said, sounding more like her real self than she had in months.

"Jessie!" her father shouted. When she didn't answer at once, his voice rose anxiously. "Jessica Kettel, where have you gone?"

When she still didn't answer—the heavy wooden platform was bobbing closer again—her father cried out in greater alarm.

"Jessie! What's wrong? Answer me now!"

This time she shouted back. "It's okay, Dad, I'm right here. I'm coming and I'm perfectly fine."

TWO

None of them—none of the children, that is—had wanted to come on this seaside adventure. How could they want to come when they were not even consulted?

"We're leaving tomorrow," their father had announced at dinner. "You'll need shorts and suits. We're going to the ocean."

The ocean! No one had been there before. No one had even thought of going.

"Which one?" Julia asked.

"The great Atlantic, of course."

"Mom's coming, right?" Jonathan had inquired suspiciously, because the trip was so sudden, not at all the way she did things.

"No. She has to work." She was in fact still at work right then.

"Then why are we going?"

"We need something different."

You mean you *need something different*, Jessie had thought. Her parents were on edge. She felt rather than saw it—a low buzz of discontent—and kept it to herself. She did not, these days, tell all that was in her mind. She would not lower herself by complaining, either, as Julia was doing now in the dingy yellow kitchen of their rented house:

"Dad, this place is terrible! It smells!"

"That's enough!" He slammed his hand on the counter, rattling a line of rusty canisters near the stove. "Look, my intention is to move us into this shack, whatever we think of it. I need all of you to help. Time is of the essence. Night cometh on cat feet."

Julia cast her eyes upward. "Dad! Get a handle. You sound like a crazy person sometimes!"

They lugged in duffels, scrubbed out the gangrenous fridge, sponged off the counters, and emptied drawers littered with mouse droppings. The upstairs windows had to be pried open by brute force and propped up with old paperbacks so the fresh sea wind could blow through. Even then an unhealthy stink hung in the air.

"Mildew," their father said. "And a dead mouse or two. The reek will clear out. Julia? You take the room at the top of the stairs."

"Oh, thank you! I was hoping for that one."

"Jessie and Jonathan will share the big room with the beautiful view at the end of the hall."

They turned on him together.

"Are you out of your mind?"

"No way!"

He gave them a steely smile and added: "And I, without

complaint, will take the small, dark cavern in the middle. Hmm-mm, a former closet from the looks."

Jessie was appalled. "I can't share a room with Jonathan. How can I? He's a mess. He goes to bed at nine o'clock. This is totally insane."

"It may be, but that is the plan. Julia asked and I agreed. She's older now and needs space."

There was no dealing with him when he spoke that way. Next he instructed the girls to make the beds, in a tone so maddening to Jessie (whereas Julia went off like an angel to find the linen closet) that she sat on the stairs and screamed. Just screamed!

"Jessie, come on. You're too old for that." Her father paused over her. "Jonathan needs you. He'll feel safer if there's someone in the room. You know how he wakes up at night in the dark."

"So *you* sleep with him!"

"I may be working late. With the light on. I'm writing something."

"You're always writing something."

"Well, now I may be writing something else. Did you know I've been here before?"

"Where, this house?"

"Not *here*. In town."

"You never told us."

"It was years ago. Now, if you'll please help Julia with the beds, I'll get Jonathan out from underfoot. We need groceries and supplies. I'll take him with me to the store. You'll be finished in no time, and then . . ." Jessie felt the weight of his considering eyes. "Then you'll have an hour to yourself before dinner. Is that a pond through the reeds, possibly in need of exploration?" His hand brushed the top of her head.

"How did you know it was there?"

"I remember it. Quicksand Pond. I used to row around out there with a friend."

"Dad! You never said. Is that why we came here?"

"Of course not."

When Jessie looked up, she saw that his attention had moved away. With compressed lips, he was gazing at Jonathan across the room. Something was about to happen. A storm was about to break.

It came with a wail; Jonathan was in tears. He'd been listening to their conversation. Hearing that he was to be taken away, removed without consent like a small child, he'd decided to push back.

"I'm not leaving," he wept to his father. "I can make my own bed."

"Well, of course, by all means, stay if you must."

"I want to explore the pond with Jessie! I don't want to go to the store."

"All right, but . . . I was thinking we might buy you a present, a little reward for being such a helpful fellow," Jessie heard her father say with expert diplomacy as they walked downstairs.

"I don't want a present."

"Oh well, I guess not, then."

"Like what kind of present?"

"I don't know. What do you want? How about bug spray?"

"Bug spray! Why do I want that? You want that."

"No, you want it," Jessie heard her father say. "You want it to knock out and capture rare and possibly undocumented bugs to add to your famous collection."

"But I don't have a famous collection."

"But you will, you will. After a few weeks in this place."

The screen door slammed.

When they had driven off, Jessie made her bed with the sheets and blankets Julia found in a cupboard at the top of the stairs. Then she went to her father's tiny room, where the bed looked too narrow for even a child. She was just tucking in the blanket when Julia's voice came down the hall.

"Are you done? I made Jonathan's bed. If you want, you can move in with me."

"That's all right." The idea of rooming with Julia and all her fake niceness seemed far more unbearable.

"I'm going to try walking to the beach," Julia said. "Maybe we can get reception down there. Have you tried your cell?"

"No."

"So get it and let's go."

"No thanks. I'm staying here."

"Oh, come on. It'll be fun. Don't be a rat."

"I'm not a rat. I just don't want to go."

"Why don't you ever want to do anything anyone else wants to do?" Julia said. "You're the most impossible person. Even Mother says so."

"Actually, I'm quite a nice person. She only said that because I don't always do what she wants."

"Well, I'll go by myself."

Julia marched down the stairs and went outside, letting the screen door slam like a rude word.

"Tell Dad where I am so he doesn't worry," she called back with another maddening show of thoughtfulness.

"Tell him yourself! I won't be here!" Jessie bellowed. She went down the hall to the room she and Jonathan would somehow occupy together and looked out the window.

The pond was there, a shadowy map of shallows and depths. From this vantage its colors were darker, navy blue and maroon. The view was extensive and revealed new details: a tiny island out in the water shaped like a haystack; the roof of what looked to be an enormous house lurking behind bushes far up one shore. Directly below her the furry back of some mysterious creature slipped silently through the reeds.

Jessie went downstairs and out the front door.

Their cottage lay at the end of a long dirt road that wound uphill through overgrown pastures. Julia's figure appeared at intervals moving up this track toward the main road. Jessie waited until her sister was out of sight before turning toward the pond. She followed her first path through the brush to the place on the bank.

The strange platform was still there, floating quite close now. She had only to stretch out a foot to draw it in. With a wary toe she tested it. A moment later she stepped out on it, grasping a clump of cattails for balance.

The wooden planks could not support her and sank under the water. Jessie leaped for dry land but too late. Her new leather sneakers were soaked and she was wet to her ankles.

The minute she was off it, the platform sprang to the surface, as if teasing her to try again. She took off her sneakers and did. This time she stepped slowly, keeping her weight even, and was better supported. She steadied herself with the reeds and saw how she could propel the raft (for this is what it seemed to be) by grabbing the bushy stems and pulling herself between them.

The pond surged warm and dark over her bare feet when she tipped to one side. But she was determined, and progressed away from the bank into deeper water. After several minutes the reeds came to an end and she could go no farther. She stood gazing out across the pond's open surface. Behind her the place she'd set out from was lost in greenery.

And I am lost too, Jessie thought. No one who hadn't seen her go off would know she was here. For a long time she stood that way, content to be woven into the silver-green fabric of the pond.

A cry echoed across the water. Or was it a laugh? Far up the shore a long-legged figure leaped away through the reeds. A marsh bird, she thought, though it looked almost human. Afterward silence spread around her, as if everything was pausing to listen. Then the murmuring symphony of aquatic noises began again: husky rattles, amphibious croaks, the drone of unseen insects. Underneath it all came a low, drumming thunder from the direction of the sand embankment at the pond's end.

That was the ocean. The great Atlantic, her father had called it. Beneath her feet the heavy wooden platform rose and fell on invisible currents. A hoarse cackle sounded overhead. She looked up to see three shiny black birds shoot past, their searchlight eyes scanning the shoreline ahead.

By now Julia would be there, walking along the sand, waving her phone over her head, trying to locate a place where the signal kicked in. Julia was an important hub person in her group back home. She connected to a network of friends, and friends of friends, who stayed continuously in touch. Hour by hour Julia received news from these contacts and passed it along. Minute by minute she reported on her own life and was reported back to.

Jessie had friends, but they would have been surprised to hear from her. She was always a little out of things at home, never the first person, or even the tenth, to know what was happening. Even now her phone was not in her pocket. It was back in the cottage in a duffel bag on the floor of her room.

A raw sea wind cut through the reeds. The sun had dropped low on the horizon and threatened soon to slide out of sight. Night was on the march. Already the water around her was veiled in purple shadow. Jessie edged across the raft, grasped a clump of reeds, and began to pull herself toward shore.

In the half-light the pond's vegetation seemed to curl around her, snarling the raft in leafy clumps. She lost track

of the route she'd taken to come out, and stopped to listen for the ocean. But the wind had risen, and the sound
was drowned out by rattling cattails. A slow wave of fear
broke through her, then a grim recognition of how ridiculous she was: to be caught in such a place, only yards from
shore, when she was the one so determined to get away. She
grasped a reedy clump and yanked herself onward.

Dark had fallen when at last she found the bank. She
barely recognized her landing place. When the raft hit shore,
she leaped off, grabbed up her sneakers, and rushed for
the house. With relief she saw that the car was there. The
shoppers had returned. She heard pots banging inside the
brightly lit kitchen and went in that way, by the back door.
She intended to say nothing about where she'd been, but:

"Look at Jessie!" Jonathan shrieked the instant she
appeared. "Did you fall in, Jessie? I guess you fell in."

When she looked down, she saw that her legs were
streaked with mud right up to the bottom of her shorts, and
that her sneakers were too wet to look new ever again. The
mark of the pond was most certainly on her.

THREE

Someone's out on the pond," Henrietta said from her command post at the bedroom window.

"Well, imagine that! Come along, Miss Cutting; time to finish your milk." Sally Parks from the HomeTouch Agency was quite up to dealing with wayward old ladies.

"Someone on a raft," Henrietta said, pushing the binoculars closer against her watery eyes. "I believe it is a child."

"And who else would it be? Who else but a child?"

Sally had put a sleeping drug in the milk, as suggested by the doctor. She wanted Henrietta to hurry up and drink it and settle down for the night.

"I'll tell you one thing, you wouldn't catch me out on a raft," Sally said. "Not in a hundred years."

"I'm sure I wouldn't," Henrietta replied. "You would have sunk it long before that."

"Beg your pardon?"

"It takes lightness to ride a raft," Henrietta said. She lowered the binoculars and glanced across at Sally's meaty shape. "Lightness," she repeated, "in both body and mind."

"Well, that's a nice thing to say! Let's have none of your insults now. Drink up the rest of your milk, dear. It'll do you good."

"I don't like milk," Henrietta said, with her eyes screwed back to the binoculars. "I prefer cranberry juice."

"That surprises me," Sally Parks countered ably. "Surprises me no end. It was just last night, I believe, that you preferred milk to cranberry juice. And I kindly went down and got it for you. Didn't I do that?"

"Did not," said Henrietta.

"Did so."

Henrietta swiveled her binoculars away from the raft, up toward the other end of the pond, where a flurry of movement had caught her eye.

"There goes that wild pond girl running home," she reported. "She's late for dinner, I'd say."

"Hah, what dinner?" Sally said, glancing out. "She's one of those Carrs at the end of the pond. The life they lead is a public shame. Come along now, Miss Cutting. Put away those binoculars. We haven't got all night."

This came out with a distinctly testy edge. Sally Parks had the patience of Job, heaven knew, but in the newspaper that morning she'd read about a television show she wanted to watch. It came on at nine p.m.

Henrietta was unmoved. She'd turned her sights back down the pond again. "That child on the raft out there doesn't know ponds," she went on. "She's splashing along like a drunken sailor, scaring things. She won't see anything that way."

Sally stepped forward. "Miss Cutting! I don't mean to rush you, but the doctor has said you must drink your milk. When you don't, you know what happens."

"What?" said Henrietta, still gazing through the window.

"Why, you don't sleep well," Sally said. "You're up all night with those terrible dreams. Now, here is your milk. Shall I help you drink it?"

Sally raised the glass rather threateningly. These bedtime wrangles were turning into a problem. They could go on for hours of coaxing and pleading.

"Oh! Let me be!"

"There now, another sip," Sally said, snatching the binoculars away and putting them out of sight under Henrietta's chair.

"Oh! Give them back!"

"Here's the rest, dear." Sally handed her the glass and stood by while she drank. Then she drew the old woman to her feet and ushered her firmly across the floor to her bed, paying not the least attention to her complaints.

The medication had a fast reaction. In no more than ten minutes Henrietta's resistance began to give way. Her long, spare body, still strong for its eighty-some years, relaxed under the coverlet. Her head fell back on the pillow.

"That's it," said Sally Parks, unhooking Henrietta's glasses deftly from the backs of her ears and placing them on the bedside table. "You just lie quiet now, honey. Think about that child on the raft. You grew up around here, didn't you? I'll bet you had a raft when you were young. I'll bet you were out there, full of your sass, tearing up and down the pond."

"No, I wasn't!" Henrietta would have said if only she could. The thought was there in her head, but her lips wouldn't work anymore. The milk had gotten to them.

No, I wasn't tearing up and down. I was poling along slow and silent, moving like a shadow through the reeds. I was listening and watching. There's nothing like a raft for sneaking up on things.

In the midst of this explanation, it suddenly seems to Henrietta Cutting that she's released from Sally's grip. She is lifted by a great gush of air, swept out the window, and flown down to the surface of the pond, where she finds herself poling along across open water, just as she used to.

There's her house with the high-dormered roof, where her family came every summer, down from Providence. There are her father and mother, and her nurse, Ella. There are her two dogs! What were their names? Oh yes, Gypsy and Sam. There she is, riding on her raft, the one she made with her own hands, hammered together so well that it never fell apart. It was always waiting for her, summer after summer, in some niche of pond bank. A miracle, when you thought of it, lasting through those blustery winters.

"Though I do recall how I took pains to stow it away before we left every fall," Henrietta muses. Half of her, it seems, is floating on the raft, while the other half looks down from some place in time slightly above and beyond.

"I'd haul it out with a rope onto the bank just below the

Coopers' cottage, where the land curves in behind a rock. I thought it'd be safe there from the north wind."

Safe.

Suddenly Henrietta sees, as if it really were before her eyes, the tall embankment below the Coopers' that announced the beginning of the ocean beach. She sees the small, haystack-shaped rock where an eagle once tried to build a nest. (It was blown away!) She sees her father on shore, waving and calling:

"Come home, Henny! There's a storm on the way."

She's stayed out too long. Deep-purple clouds are bearing down on the pond. Waves are splashing up over her feet. There isn't much you can do when the wind starts to blow that hard off the ocean. Except kneel down and paddle. Paddle fast with your hands.

"Get down, Henny. Work your way over here!" The wind roars past her ears, carrying her father's words.

How he'd loved her. She felt the warmth of it still, after all these years. He would've jumped in and swum out to rescue her if he'd had to. That day she'd paddled in on her own, made it through the waves to where he waited on shore. He'd pulled her onto dry land and wrapped his arms around her. "My strong girl," he said. "I have you. Safe."

None of this does Henrietta say or show the least evidence of to Sally Parks. But it is in her mind, a mind surrounded now by encroaching borders of age, so that its shores are reedy and no longer always visible to those around her; a mind upon which mists rise and depart at unpredictable moments, where memories fly up like swans off water and thoughts ride out alone across a wide blue surface.

Like a child on a raft. Like a girl on a raft long ago and at this moment.

So long ago, Henrietta thinks in silent surprise. *And here it is, coming around again.* She sees time in her mind as a slow revolving globe.

So I am responsible. I have called out this child! Henrietta concludes. She's flown up off the pond and is back in her own bedroom now.

Except she doesn't know how to go quietly on a raft. What she needs is a pole. Oh, where is my pole? I must look to see where I last laid it!

It wasn't ten minutes more before Sally Parks was tiptoeing out of the room, closing the door, and heading downstairs to the kitchen, while the old lady snored herself into oblivion. And not a moment too soon. That television program was just coming on.

FOUR

nyone would suppose that with an entire pond at their door and an ocean down the road, water would be the least problem in the Kettels' little vacation cottage. Just the opposite; they had to think about it all the time. Water pressure was so low that the shower delivered only the feeblest trickle. Toilets belched and backed up. Faucets spit, then stopped. Spit and stopped.

It was easy to see "why this dump wasn't already rented," as Julia whispered to Jessie out of earshot of their father. He called them wimps and babies for complaining. "You've been living too long in the lap of luxury!" he blustered.

On the phone from Pittsburgh, their mother suggested that the entire house, built so close to a marsh, was probably in violation of federal codes. Environmental law was her specialty.

"It's not a marsh," snapped Richard Kettel, speaking into the plastic receiver of the only telephone in the house, an old-fashioned rotary-dial model. "It's a lovely old pond, and in case you're wondering, we're all happy as clams here."

"Well, I hope you're not drinking the water."

"We are!"

"Your mother doesn't like my choice of vacation destinations," he told the children after he'd hung up. "She seems to think our lives are in danger."

"You don't have the best track record in that department," Julia observed. "Remember that raging river we had to swim when you got us lost in Montana?"

"That was the guide, not me, and it was hardly a raging river."

"What about the time we were sailing on Lake Arthur and you ran us into the mud, and night was coming and we had to call the lake patrol to get us out?" Jonathan said.

Their father heaved a sigh and did not reply.

Water was not the only problem.

"The electrical system is shot," their father admitted after the second blackout. "Watch out for sparks when you plug anything in. And no more hair dryers." He looked at the girls. "And don't run the toaster oven for longer than two minutes."

"Are we allowed to use the blender?" Julia asked sweetly. She was known to live on fruit and veggie smoothies at home.

"There *is* no blender," Jonathan pointed out.

"Brilliant," she said, flattening him with a look. The Julia of old was clearly on the rise.

There was no television, either—that went without saying. No radio. Julia had music on her smartphone, but she didn't allow anyone else to use her earphones. "And I can't download anything new!" she complained. "I'm listening to the same stuff over and over."

"So live with it," her father told her. "Personally, I think it's a relief to have silence for a change. And darkness. Have you been out to look at the stars? Here we are, face-to-face with the natural world. We should take advantage of it. There are candles in the bottom drawer of the hall chest, in case of emergency."

"This whole place is an emergency," Julia muttered.

"We're getting to find out what it was like to live a hundred years ago," Jessie proposed.

"Like in the Dark Ages!" Jonathan crowed, which made everyone laugh.

For the most part, though, the Kettel family was not together laughing. By the end of the first week, they were not together at all, except by necessity at breakfast and dinner. Almost immediately they found themselves swept into different channels.

Julia met up with a group her age on the beach—the erratic nature of wireless connection was a great conversation starter—and after that spent most of her time there with them. A boy in the group had a car and would come by shyly to pick her up. Julia, who considered shyness to be a defect in men, called him the Silent Lamb and did not give him any credit for these rides.

Jonathan and his father visited various haunts, like the fish docks at the harbor and the local hardware store, where they bought fuses and mousetraps and pieces of wire for mending the screens.

Then Jonathan also found friends—especially Philip, who had a swimming pool and invited Jonathan over nearly every day to play Marco Polo.

"Why anyone needs a swimming pool in their backyard when they live three minutes from a beach, I don't know," their father said. "It's the worst kind of excess."

He remembered the town as a simple country place where fishermen chugged around the sleepy harbor and milkmen delivered fresh cream and eggs from neighboring farms. Since then it had apparently fallen into the hands of the idle rich. With Jonathan away, he spent his time alone, reading on the partly shaded back porch of the cottage. He drove to the general store in the village for groceries, visited the tiny library there and the old graveyard on the town green. Sometimes he could be seen writing by hand on a yellow pad. He'd forgotten how he used to do that, he said, how close a simple pencil could bring a person to his own words.

"Are you working on your novel?" Jessie asked, coming into the house alone late one afternoon. At home he'd been writing a novel, they all knew, writing it for years, with no end in sight. Jessie suspected this was one of the issues between her parents. Her mother was a person of swift and decisive action. She said she would do a thing, made a plan, and carried it out. Richard Kettel was a hedger and a circler.

"Just jotting down some notes," he answered vaguely. "This place is great for background. The old parts, I mean, that have been here for years. This is where I started writing, you know, the summer I was here. I've had it in my mind to come back for a long time. Simplicity and quiet. What've you been doing?"

"Oh, walking around."

"Walking around where?"

"Just . . . around."

It sounded false even to Jessie's ears, and it was. The truth was, she'd gone back to the raft, had been out on it several more times without telling anyone. Why the big secret? Perhaps it was Julia. Julia might have laughed. She might have said: "A raft? Grow up! The beach is where everything happens around here. Everyone who's anyone is down there."

Which was true. Jessie wasn't a loner. She wanted to be popular. She knew she should be down there fitting in, leaving an impression, proving what an interesting person she was.

She knew, but . . . that summer something stronger pulled her toward the pond. She went to it whenever there was a moment to slip away. Stealthily she stepped out on the raft's sodden planks and pushed off from the bank. She'd make for the edge of the cattails. There she'd stand for an hour breathing in the place, listening and watching for what lived there unseen. A frog stalking flies. Stick-leg bugs that walked on water. A mother duck and her fleet of tiny, corklike babies.

She would have gone farther out, but the raft was too heavy to paddle by hand. Beyond the reeds she'd have needed an oar or a stick to push along with. Since nothing like that was available, she had to settle for staying close to shore.

But that was about to change.

FIVE

arly morning. Everyone was asleep. The sun, just up, filtered through the reeds. The pond lay still in a mantle of mist. Jessie was picking her way, barefoot, toward the raft when a broad ray of sunlight broke through onto the ground. There, lying amidst weeds, almost invisible unless you happened to be stepping right over it, was a long, slender wooden pole.

She stopped. How had this come to be here? It was as if someone had read her mind and left the pole for her to find. She bent closer, and as fast as the mystery had arisen, it faded and was solved. The pole was nothing more than a prop for the old clothesline. A second prop, actually. Another just like it was attached to the line in their cottage's backyard.

When the line sagged in the middle from too much wet laundry, you propped it up with this long notched pole so the clothes wouldn't drag on the ground. Her father had explained it, though no one in the family had yet hung out even a pair of socks. They weren't using the line except occasionally for wet beach towels. They took their dirty clothes up the road to a Laundromat. Or rather, her father took them. He didn't mind. He was used to doing the wash at home. It was restful, he said. He could read undisturbed.

Whatever the pole was meant to be, Jessie saw it in a new light now. She took it down to the raft and pushed away from the bank like a gondolier. She planted the notched end on the pond's sticky bottom and pushed again. The raft glided out between the reeds.

The water that morning rose only to the soles of her feet. Perhaps the raft had begun to dry out. The weather had been continuously bright and hot. She poled awkwardly at first. The trick was a stabbing and thrusting rhythm that took practice. After some tipping, and once losing her balance and falling all the way in, she reached the outer limits of the reeds.

Without a pause she pushed off and sent the raft coasting out onto the pond's glassy surface. The mist parted and she was alone, the only human alive on this blue summer morning. She passed a solitary stone chimney on the far shore where a cottage about the size of their own must once have stood. A cement foundation glistened in the sun like a child-size basketball court.

She came up on the haystack-shaped island. It was really only a big granite rock with a coating of bird droppings on the crown, like snow on an Alpine peak. A pile of sticks clung to one side. A nest? She poled past.

A grand house ringed with porches rose to view on shore,

the same house whose distant roof she'd glimpsed before. She was amazed she'd come so far. When she turned to look back down the pond, it took a moment to recognize the gray smudge of her own cottage, tiny against the land. Quicksand Pond was larger than it appeared from shore. She felt vulnerable suddenly, too much on view, and brought the raft in closer to the reedy edge.

From an inland place a dog began to bark. She went by a narrow wooden dock built out over the marsh grass. A line of buoys bobbed near shore. She was more skillful with the pole now, able to glide along smoothly with hardly any splashing. When she came upon a congregation of seagulls dozing on yet another decrepit dock, she passed them so quietly that not a single bird was disturbed.

The alluring bend in the pond rose in front of her. Jessie decided to go around it, take a quick look, and turn back. By now breakfast would be under way in the Kettel kitchen. Her father had found wild blueberries on sale at a local fruit stand. He'd promised to make them blueberry pancakes last night after another uncomfortable phone call from their mother. ("You talk to her, I have nothing more to say," he'd snapped, holding the receiver out to Julia.)

The bend was really a bush-infested peninsula, a place where sand from the distant beach had been washed up in a ridge that reached out like a dark arm into the pond. Jessie took the raft around it. On the other side she heard voices coming through reeds, the low growl of a man's voice and the higher tones of someone younger.

"You come over here and get what's coming to you."

"Leave me alone. You're crazy."

"I'll fix you this time."

"I didn't do anything. Keep away from me."

Jessie heard the sound of a slap. Dimly, through the brush, she saw the shapes of two people struggling. The smaller figure gave a short, smothered cry, pulled away, and ran around the corner of a broken-down farmhouse. The man followed with a lazy, loping gallop, as if he knew it was only a matter of time before he'd catch up.

Jessie stood frozen on the raft. For a long moment there was only the gentle lap of the pond around her. Then the running figure of a girl shot out from behind the house like a small, frantic bird and came toward the pond. The man appeared five seconds later, moving faster.

"Get back here!"

"Leave me alone!"

The girl plowed into the reeds at the edge of the pond and began to beat her way through. As she waded deeper into the water, she began a desperate hitching and wallowing motion that was half swimming, half running on the pond's muddy floor.

The man didn't attempt to follow her there. He detoured to a short dock at the water's edge and jumped into a skiff tied up there. He flung off the rope, shipped the oars, and began to row with experienced quickness across open water toward where the girl had entered the reeds. She was still floundering in them, pushing her way through. Jessie suddenly understood that she was trying to cut through to the other side of the sand peninsula. This idea must have occurred to the man in the skiff at almost the same moment, because he backed his oars and turned the boat sharply. His intention now was to round the sand spit and intercept the girl on the other side. His back toward Jessie, he began to row straight at her.

Jessie went into action. She poled the raft backward, away from the floundering girl, away from the angry man, who had already closed the distance between them by half and was coming across the water at a horrifying speed. Jessie rounded the bend, poled harder, and, gasping for breath, drove the raft deep into a narrow alley between some reeds. She turned and drew the reeds down to make a curtain around herself. There she cowered, and covered her ears against the sounds of the inevitable capture. A half minute went by. Then another half minute.

Jessie lifted her hands off her ears. No sound of capture came. Instead, another noise was filtering into her hiding place: the watery slurp of someone moving stealthily through the reeds behind her. She whirled around.

The girl. With slow and by now very tired hitches and wallows, she came toward the raft.

"Shhh. Let me on." Her face was dark red and bathed in sweat. She raised a finger to her lips and crawled on board. The raft, overweighted, sank under the water. Screened by reeds, submerged above their ankles, the two crouched side by side without speaking.

The skiff appeared around the bend, a horizontal flicker through the upright reeds. It passed their hiding place, thrust forward with dangerous, knifelike stabs as the man stroked powerfully through the still pond water.

"Come out of there, you little sneak!"

Under Jessie the raft wobbled. The girl was shifting her weight. Or was she trembling?

"Are you all right?" Jessie whispered.

"Shhh! He can hear like a dog."

They crouched motionless, in silence.

The skiff shot past going back the way it had come, toward the bend.

"You're going to get it when I catch you!" There was a tone to the man's voice that made Jessie want to stop breathing, to stop even the blink of her eyelids in case he heard them. Her body locked down. Only her eyes kept pace with the flickering course of the boat.

"You'll be sorry," the voice snarled. "You don't know how sorry you'll be."

He went around the bend and out of sight. The girl beside her relaxed her stiff posture. She stood up lightly.

"He'll stop looking now," she whispered.

"How do you know?"

"That's what he always says when he quits." Wet strands of black hair were stuck to her thin face. One cheek was streaked with mud.

"What happened?" Jessie whispered.

The girl shrugged. "He says I stole ten bucks off him."

"But you didn't?"

"Sure I did, like I always do."

"Oh."

"I told him he'd lost it somewhere when he was out last night. He just didn't believe me. He should've believed me." The girl looked directly at Jessie for the first time. "I mean, how else am I going to get money off him?"

"I don't know."

"Right. That's the only way."

By now the girl had climbed down off the raft and was standing once more on the pond's bottom, water up to her waist. The raft, with only Jessie on it, bobbed up again to the surface.

"You should fix this thing so it floats better," the girl said. "That big crosspiece on top is waterlogged."

"It is?"

"Sure. If you just took it off, that side would come up and the whole raft would float better. I bet even two people could get on it then."

"Is that your name?" Jessie asked. The girl was wearing a chain necklace with the letters *T-e-r-r-i* in gold script, hanging like a charm below the hollow of her throat.

"Terri," Terri said. "In case you can't read."

"Well, I can," Jessie said. They glared at each other.

Terri smoothed her name charm with the tips of two fingers. Her scornful expression softened. "Your raft's floating pretty good now that I'm off it," she said.

Jessie nodded. "It brought me this far, anyway. I should probably get going before it totally sinks. Also I'm late for breakfast. My whole family will be wondering where I am."

"You're renters, aren't you."

"Yes."

"Well, see you around." Terri plunged off through the reeds. Not heading in the direction of her house, going in the opposite direction. Jessie gave the raft a shove toward open water. Then she stuck the pole in and brought it up short.

"What will you do now?" she called in a low voice.

"Hang out somewhere." Terri didn't look back. She kept moving through the reeds toward shore. "I've got to wait till night, then I can go home. He goes off at night. By morning he's forgotten what happened. Or come to his senses, one or the other."

"Is he . . ." Jessie hesitated. "Is he, you know, related to you?"

"What do you think? He's my father." Terri glanced back at her.

"Sorry. I mean . . ."

"He gets mad sometimes, that's all. Otherwise he's okay. It's no problem. I can handle it."

She began to move away from Jessie again.

"Hey, wait! You can hang out with me for a while, if you want."

"Why?" Terri kept going.

"Because." Jessie hunted for an answer. "Because I need to fix this raft. You're right. It doesn't float too well."

The girl slowed, considering. She glanced in the direction of her house. Other figures had now appeared in the yard. More yelling had started up. She slicked her dark hair back from her face with both hands.

"Thanks but no thanks. You can fix your own raft."

"Are you sure?" Jessie asked. "What about . . ."

"All you need is a crowbar," Terri said. She looked over her shoulder at her house again.

"A crowbar. What's that?"

"Don't you even know what a crowbar is?"

"No."

"You renters are scary," Terri said. "Where did you find this raft, anyhow? I know you didn't build it." She began to slosh back.

"It was just in the water by the bank. Near our house."

"That's strange. Do you know how strange that is? There's never been a raft on this pond that I know of."

"Have you lived here for long?"

"I was born here," Terri said.

"Well, come and jump on. It's getting too deep to walk."

So Terri got up on the raft again, which immediately sank ankle-deep in the water. This made it hard, but not impossible, to pole along. They took turns, keeping close to the tall reeds so they wouldn't be seen from shore. The yelling in Terri's yard faded. In the distance the solitary stone chimney rose into view, a landmark that Jessie could steer by.

"Our house is straight across from that."

"I know where it is."

They came up on the haystack-shaped rock dusted with bird droppings.

"That's not a nest. It's an old duck blind," Terri said, as if she knew Jessie's question. "Duck hunters used to come here."

"But they don't anymore?"

"The reeds have gotten too thick to drag a boat through. Anyway, you know, this pond is haunted."

"Haunted by who?"

It was then that Terri Carr told about the Peckham boys. She grinned her toothy grin and told about the drowned cows, and the terrible murder of the young girl's parents while she slept upstairs so long ago.

Jessie listened ("She still lives here") and gazed with uneasy interest at the roof of the big house that rose through the bushes on shore.

"Want to come in for breakfast?" she asked when they arrived at the landing place near the Kettel cottage. "My dad is making blueberry pancakes."

Terri shook her head. "Thanks for the ride." She stepped ashore and turned to leave.

"Wait!" Jessie said. "I thought you were going to hang out here for a while. I thought you were going to help fix this raft."

"I never said that."

"Yes, you did. You said we could use a crowbar."

"So? It's going to take a lot more than a crowbar to get this old thing floating again."

"Okay, then tell me. What should I do?"

"I can't tell you stuff like that. I bet you wouldn't even know enough to use galvanized nails."

"I wouldn't," Jessie agreed. "What are galvanized nails?"

Terri's eyes flicked over her.

"Listen, you don't have to make up some reason to invite

me over. It's not like I need to be here or anything. Whatever you saw, it's not really like that."

"I know."

Terri shrugged. "Well, I'll think about it. I have a lot going on right now. I don't know if I can fit this in."

She strode away, batting the reeds aside.

But she was back the next day.

SIX

n the olden times of farms and duck hunting, before city vacationers began to crowd the shore, the Cuttings had owned the only real summer home in town. It was a house with three porches looking off in three directions. Verandas, Henrietta Cutting's mother had called them. She was a Lee from the South. One veranda was for the sea view, one was for the pond view, and one looked up the road toward the village center, where a white church steeple rose above the trees like a ship's mast.

Some days Henrietta awoke remembering these views as they had been: long, unimpeded vistas across green fields to the sea; the gray ribs of stone walls dividing up the land; cows, sheep, and haycocks dotting pastures far-off and near.

Then, when she went to her bedroom window and looked out, she got a shock. Everything was changed! It was unimaginably transformed. A whole countryside had been uprooted and turned about, subtracted and added, so that she might as well have been in China as in the seaside cor-ner of the world she'd lived in most of her life. Which was what she said to Sally Parks, who was drawing water in the bathtub, changing the towels, locating clean underwear, and attempting to get an orderly start on the day.

"Might as well be in China!"

"Come along, Miss Cutting. Time to wash up."

Might as well be but was not. Henrietta knew this a second later because she saw the pond. It seemed to have filled in around the edges during the night. She didn't recall there being so many reeds yesterday. It was the same pond, though, with the same little haystack-shaped island in the middle. And being the same, it anchored the land around it. Whatever strange vegetal mutations had erupted during the night, whatever herds of cattle had been swallowed up or pastures or barns erased, the pond was still there, holding its own.

Holding on to Henrietta Cutting, too. She knew where she was most of the time. After breakfast she looked around for her binoculars. Sally Parks handed them over pleasantly enough. She could get through the morning newspaper while Henrietta spent a happy hour spying out the window.

"What's happening out there today?" Sally asked, flipping a page with a licked finger. "Any murders, muggings, governmental hanky-panky?"

"Nothing like that," Henrietta said.

"That cousin of yours called last night after you were in bed," Sally said. "She can't come up in mid-August like she thought. Her boys start school then. When I was a girl, in Maine, we didn't start school till late September. That was left over from the old farming days, when kids were needed for the harvest. Probably changed by now."

Henrietta was leaning forward in her narrow wing chair, binoculars raised, panning the countryside. She'd largely forgotten her family, who didn't appear often enough to be of consequence. Their offspring had dropped off the screen entirely. Henrietta would have been very surprised to hear they were ever born.

"There are two children out on my raft this morning," she informed Sally presently.

"Two! Heavens to Betsy!" Sally exclaimed without looking up.

"That's good," Henrietta said. "I'll need two to do what I want them to do."

"And what is that?" Sally asked.

"Never you mind," Henrietta said craftily.

She hadn't always lived in this big house with the wraparound porches. This was the house she'd come to in the summer with her parents before . . . well, before. And had come back to later, after she got out of custody. Prison: That was how she thought of it, the time when the family court got its hands on her. She was signed away to some cousins in Philadelphia. To shut her up, Henrietta believed now. To silence her. But they hadn't wanted her. They had a family of their own. So she was hustled off to a London boarding school at the age of twelve, sent away without anyone even asking her if she wanted to go. Imagine. All the way to England.

"That's what happens when you're a child," Henrietta told Sally Parks. "You're ignored. Nobody listens to you, even when you're trying to tell them the truth."

"And what truth is that?" Sally inquired.

"That I know who did it," Henrietta said.

"Who did what?"

"Never you mind. It wasn't who they said, that I know."

Sally shook her head and went back to the newspaper. She'd heard this tiresome line of talk before. The old lady's thoughts got stuck in the past. She couldn't see how time had moved on, though you had to feel sorry for her, losing her parents in that terrible way. But that was years ago, more than seventy years!

"Would you like a cushion, Miss Cutting? If you lean forward any farther in that chair, you'll fall out of it."

Henrietta, panning the pond, gave a sudden gasp. She'd come across the lonesome form of a stone chimney on the opposite bank. Something had happened to the hunting cabin that used to be there. That *had* been there just yesterday. Had it been swept out to sea?

"Was there a big storm last night?" she inquired over her shoulder.

"Last night? No, nothing to speak of," Sally said.

"There's been a good bit of destruction outside since I last looked. A whole house has gone missing."

Henrietta knew who'd stayed there. The Cooper family. The mother had brought her children, a girl and a boy, down from Providence to rough it in the summer. The father turned up occasionally to hunt with his low-life pals. Whatever he did for a living—restaurants?—it wasn't in the same league as her father, Mr. George C. Cutting, prominent lawyer and owner of the *Providence Evening News*.

She'd come to know the Cooper children at the beach, however. Anyone who came down in the summer, whoever they were, you got to know them. Except for the townsfolk, there weren't many others around. There wasn't as much swimming in those days. Women guarded their complexions and people were afraid of currents. Many couldn't even swim. Henrietta's father taught her to swim off their private pier on the pond when she was quite young, five or six. That was the advantage of living on the pond, and of having a father who really cared to pay attention.

"I don't think the Cooper children ever learned to swim. Not either of them," Henrietta said to Sally. The thought had just occurred to her after all these years that this was why they'd been afraid to come out on her raft. "I could swim like a fish," she added with pride.

"A fish?" Sally murmured, lost in the news. "Where?"

Henrietta didn't attempt to explain. Sally Parks was not privy to the silent springs and underwater currents by which Henrietta's mind moved these days. She imagined Henrietta's thoughts spinning aimlessly in space, unconnected. In Sally's view, whatever was not visible, hearable, touchable, provable, did not exist on the face of the earth.

Henrietta, navigating the deep waters of old age, had found a broader perspective. To her, past and present were often one and the same, or so well interlaced as to be inter-changeable.

Present was the morning news, yesterday's news, and the news of many years of mornings gone by, all rolled into one: a clanking caravan of events punctuated by gunshots, plane crashes, war in desperate lands. Meanwhile, the past was happening now. Or was about to happen. It had nothing to do with the official baloney called "history." The past was personal, as close as your own shadow. You felt it sliding along behind you wherever you went: a face, an atmosphere, a shape in the dark. A memory sunk long ago in time's brack-ish water, but alive, still pulsing, always waiting to come up.

"No, I haven't forgotten," Henrietta murmured. She low-ered her eyes to the surface of the pond and experienced a glow of awareness. She would make her escape in good time. She would tell her story.

The two on the raft were girls of about the age of twelve or thirteen. Their unselfconscious, boyish movements gave them away. One was the pond girl, Henrietta was almost sure: the one who lived at the end of the pond with her "shameful family," as Sally called them. Henrietta recog-nized her wild little figure. The other girl was the child she'd seen the other day.

They'd found the poling stick but had not yet gotten the raft to float properly. It trailed along under the water, one side listing precariously. What the girls needed to do was take the big top plank off. It was waterlogged and was drag-ging down the rest.

The reason the top plank had become waterlogged, Henrietta understood with the shrewdness of one who had dealt with such problems in the past, was that this plank used to be on the raft's bottom. The raft was upside down. It had been flipped over by a windstorm or some tempestuous whirl of waves. The sodden bottom plank had become an oppressive top plank, overweighting the entire structure.

So: Remove the waterlogged plank. Find some solid pieces of lumber to put in its place. Hammer them on. (Use galvanized nails or they'd rust through in a year.) Turn the raft over so the good lumber was on the bottom again. Presto! The raft would be ready for action.

Sally Parks heard Henrietta murmuring to herself in a deranged-sounding undertone. She heard the words "Presto!" and "Action!" but assumed she'd misunderstood. Old ladies were slow and dense as molasses and never spoke in such terms.

"Can I get you some cranberry juice, Miss Cutting? And a cookie?"

Henrietta ignored this ridiculous question. She'd told the girls what to do and now she was wondering where to get the new lumber. Such things were not easy to come by. She'd have to hunt around and see what she could come up with. One time she'd found a good pine plank out in back of the Coopers' cottage. She was just dragging it off when the boy, Albert, showed up. He must have been watching her from the house.

"What d'you think you're doing?"

"Just getting this plank. Nobody wants it, do they?"

"Who says?"

"Well, it's just laying here as if nobody wanted it."

"What do you want it for?"

"I just need it." She didn't want to tell him about the raft. It was her prize possession. Her secret means of transport.

"If you tell me what it's for, we might let you have it," Albert said, not unreasonably. He was older.

She took him down to the edge of the pond and showed him the raft. It was aging by then, needing new wood in places. He asked if her parents knew what she was up to, going out on the pond by herself. How old was she, anyway?

She'd just turned twelve but didn't say.

"Of course my parents know! My father helped me build this raft. We made this poling stick too."

They'd built all kinds of things together. A doghouse for their basset, Gypsy. A bench to sit out on during warm summer evenings. A pretty cedar box for her mother's jewelry, to protect it from the salt air. They'd lined the box with special felt that made it airtight. They'd put a seal on it, and a lock. The way they'd built that box, nothing was ever going to bother those jewels. Her father had said that.

Albert thought it was funny, a father teaching a daughter how to build things.

"He doesn't have a son. I'm the only child, so he has to teach me," Henrietta remembered explaining, covering for him. That was not the reason, though. Her father had taught her because she'd wanted to learn, and because he'd believed she could.

Albert gave her the plank in the end. She took it home, cut it to the right size, and hammered it onto her raft. She used pike nails, over a foot long. By that time she'd gotten quite handy with tools. Her father's tools, they were. He had a fine set he kept in his workshop off the garage. Hammers, saws, chisels, planes, braces and drills, clamps and calipers, drawknives, slicks, even a boring machine with a whole set of different-size bits.

Afterward, after the shock of everything, she forgot the workshop. She never tried to build anything again. She knew how but kept it a secret. Girls weren't supposed to know about that anyway. In London they taught her to sew. Embroidery, crochet, hemstitch. She did it with mutiny in her heart. All the silly knotting and stitching; stuck for hours in a chair while her head buzzed like an angry fly. She came out of that school and was sent to another. And another. Nobody wanted her at home. Nobody wanted her anywhere. She lost touch with her childhood and was never allowed back.

"Have we got any lumber in the garage?" Henrietta asked Sally Parks when she came bringing lunch on a tray.

"Lumber!" Sally hooted. "What do you want that for?"

"Never you mind," Henrietta said. She looked back out the window, but by then the girls on the raft had passed on down the pond and gone out of sight.

SEVEN

When you were out on the pond back then, what were you in? A boat?" Jessie asked her father the morning of her first meeting with Terri Carr.

She was eating the wild-blueberry pancakes Terri had turned down. Her father had kept them warm for her in the oven. The others had finished breakfast and moved on: Julia to the beach with her silent chauffeur; Jonathan to the downstairs lavatory, where he stood on a stool, closely examining his tongue in the mirror over the sink.

"Purple!" he was yelling. "It's completely purple!"

"A skiff," her father answered.

"Why were you even here? Come on, tell. I know it wasn't for writing."

"Why was I here?" She saw he was embarrassed. "Well, I was hired, that's why. By a trash collection company. That was the summer I picked up people's garbage."

He sent a challenging glance across the table, as if he was afraid his daughter might find this laughable.

"Sounds like a good job," Jessie said. "Where did you live?"

"I had a room over the general store in town. I loved it, actually. No car, but that was okay. I went everywhere on a bike. It was the first time I'd been away from home on my own."

Jonathan came out of the bathroom. "I think my tonsils are purple too, but I can't see down that far. Can you look?" He stopped in front of Jessie and opened wide.

"That is so disgusting. Go away!"

When he'd retreated to the living room, Jessie said, "It must've been before you married Mom."

"Long before. I was Julia's age. No, a couple of years older."

"And you went out rowing?"

"There was a guy I worked with. We got to be friends. He lived on the pond and had a skiff. A little rowboat. We'd take it out and fish sometimes on Sundays, our day off. We never caught much."

"Who was he?" Jessie asked.

"Just a kid like me who needed a summer job. I was building up a bank account for college that fall. We lived in Boston then, and I'd answered a newspaper ad. With Mitch, this was home and the job was more like survival. The family was in rough shape. His dad had taken off when he was little. Left his mother with a bunch of kids. There was a grandfather who was in prison for some terrible crime. I remember they drove to Pennsylvania to visit him one time."

"So his name was Mitch?"

"Short for Mitchell. I've forgotten his last name. His family had owned a dairy that had long since closed down. A lot of the farms around here had gone bust by the time I got here. People were struggling to get by. I remember Mitch wore the same pair of pants all summer. A nice guy, though. Good natured. I felt sorry for him. His mother cleaned houses for the summer people. I don't know what they did in the winter when everybody went home."

"Is he still here, do you think?"

"Probably not. It was over thirty years ago." Her father paused. "I guess I could check."

"That's okay," Jessie said quickly. "I just kind of wondered."

There seemed at first to be no way to fix the raft. They had no tools, for one thing. For another, they needed new wood if they were going to replace the waterlogged plank. And the right kind of nails. And a dry place on shore to drag the raft up onto that was clear of bushes and still hidden from outside eyes. Terri was all about staying out of sight. Whether this was because of her father or some other reason, Jessie didn't know. There was a lot she didn't know about Terri in the beginning, but that didn't matter. Jessie liked her. She liked that she wasn't part of some crowd.

Terri seemed to like Jessie, too, because she began to turn up in the morning with some regularity at the Kettels' cottage. She wouldn't come in. She'd sit cross-legged on the grass a little way from the front door and wait for Jessie to come out.

"Who is that?" her father asked the first time.

"Terri," Jessie said. "She lives near here."

"Well, ask her to come in."

"She doesn't want to," Jessie said.

Julia looked out and said: "She looks weird. What's wrong with her?"

"Nothing's wrong with her," Jessie said. "She just wants to stay outside. Actually, she's a great person."

And so she seemed to Jessie. Terri was unlike the people she knew at home. For starters, Terri said what she was really thinking, even if it wasn't nice. If she didn't like something, or somebody, she said so. She didn't show off or try to prove that she was better or different. She just was who she was, and that was fine with her.

She could be quiet. Sometimes she didn't speak for an hour or more. She kept apart during these spells. She'd walk away and sit by herself, fingering the name charm on her throat and looking out at the pond. There was something about feeling that charm secure in its place around her neck that seemed to give her peace. At such times Jessie knew to let her be.

But after a while she'd come back and be loud and sarcastic. During these moods she'd tell Jessie things, information that opened her eyes. Terri knew things other people didn't. She knew what was really going on under the surface of what seemed to be going on.

"You know that old Buick your sister is riding around in with that preppy boy?"

Jessie hadn't thought of Julia's beach chauffeur as preppy. Now, thanks to Terri, she noticed his clothes and the way he combed his hair. She saw he was a type.

"Well, it's stolen," Terri said about the car. "A lot of people know. Not stolen by him. His rich parents bought it for him off a guy in town who bought it from the guy who stole it in New Hampshire. The parents were clueless. They just thought they got a good price."

"Really?"

"Don't tell your sister, though. It might leak out and get someone in trouble."

"Okay. But if everybody knows . . ."

"Not the summer people. They don't know anything. But we know, the people who live around here know. Want a Milky Way? I've got two."

Terri always had food tucked away on her somewhere. She kept soup crackers in her pockets, or crushed packages of snack cakes, or linty jelly beans. She was generous about offering to share.

"No thanks," Jessie would say. "Not right now."

Terri carried other things in her pockets too.

"I bet you've never seen one of these." She showed Jessie a black case that snapped open into a knife blade. A little button on the handle was the trigger.

"For protection," she said. "I could take somebody down if I had to."

Jessie was startled. "But you wouldn't . . ."

"No. I just know I could. If I was alone somewhere and

they came at me. I've killed rabbits with this knife, but you can do that with your bare hands."

"Why would you?"

"Kill a rabbit? Well, for one thing, they're real tasty in a stew. Have you ever had rabbit stew?"

Jessie hadn't.

"My mom used to make the best one in the world, everybody said so. You could bring her four or five rabbits and she'd have them dressed and in the pot before you could hardly blink. And that night, wow! We'd all be there for sure to eat, and so would my brothers' friends. We had good times when she was here."

"What do you mean, 'dressed'?" Jessie asked. She didn't want to ask what had happened to Terri's mother. She thought it wouldn't be polite.

"Oh, you know. Skinned, and the guts cleaned out. You need to skin a rabbit right away, soon as you can before it cools down," Terri advised. "Otherwise it gets sticky."

They'd been acquainted for several days by the time this conversation took place. The raft was still not fixed, but they'd figured out how to ride it lightly through the water with the least amount of friction. Their feet were always wet, but who cared? Jessie got to love the feel of pond water washing through her bare toes. She loved the pond's warmth in sunny, shallow places and its sudden cold in the shadows between the reeds. Splinters were a problem, though. The raft's pine boards were rough and slippery. After Jessie got a couple of big slivers in her feet, Terri took off her own rubber flip-flops and handed them to her.

"That's okay, you don't need to give me yours."

"It's no problem, just until you get some. I guess you don't need flip-flops where you live."

"It's in the city, so we don't," Jessie agreed. "What about you?"

"I'll just use a pair of my brother's. He won't care." Terri grinned. "Long as I don't tell him."

Sometimes they pulled the raft out into deeper water and swam off it for a whole afternoon. Those were the best days because they were so free. There was no one to tell them what to do or when to do it. Hours passed, the sun shone, and for Jessie, at least, there was the blissful sense of having no one nearby to call her home.

"You're so lucky you can always do what you want," she told Terri. "I mean, no one worries about you, do they?"

Terri shrugged. "Yeah, I'm pretty much on my own, if that's what you want to call it."

Some days were spent in exploration. The pond had so many inlets and outlets, nooks and crannies. They poked along the ocean end of it, where the babble of children playing on the beach came through the thick brush.

"Did you swim on that beach when you were little?" Jessie asked.

Terri said, "Are you kidding?"

They went up the shore in the other direction, past the old Carr house with its messy backyard.

"Is your dad there?" Jessie asked nervously.

"When his pickup isn't there, you know he's not home," Terri said. "Unless he got a ride with someone. Sometimes he fools you."

They went to a mudflat that was filled with sunning turtles. Terri caught a couple of young ones and let them scrabble around on the raft, looking for escape. Jessie was relieved when she tossed them back in the water. They looked so small and desperate.

They poled up an inlet to a field where a gray fox lived in a burrow, raising a litter. Terri knew how to call the kits with a high, yipping cry. There were four, or perhaps five. It was hard to tell because they were shy and would not come out for long. The next day, at Terri's suggestion, Jessie brought a loaf of sandwich bread she'd sneaked out of the kitchen. They tore off pieces and threw them near the foxes' burrow. The kits appeared at once—five!—and fought fiercely among themselves to get their share. When they'd eaten everything, they glanced over their shoulders at their strange human feeders (Jessie thought she and Terri must appear this way to them) and cried out for more like demanding children.

"So cute!" Jessie exclaimed, but Terri warned, "Don't get too close. The mother's in the bushes. She'll come out and go after you if she thinks you're bothering them. There's nothing nastier than a mother fox watching out for her kits. Except maybe a mother bear."

By then Jessie knew what she'd suspected was true: Mitch was Terri's father. She knew because that's what Terri called him.

"I've got to go home now to help Mitch fix the porch," Terri would say. Or, "Jerry crashed his truck again, so Mitch took him to work." Jerry was one of her brothers, who worked on and off in an auto repair shop. Her other brother showed up only once in a while, an event no one looked forward to.

"It's usually when he's broke," Terri said in disgust. "Then everyone gets in a fight."

"Why do you call your father Mitch?" Jessie asked.

"It's just what everyone calls him."

"But he's your dad."

"So what? He'd probably laugh his head off if we called him that."

Terri's father was the same person her father had gone fishing with in the old days. He was the poor, good-natured kid who'd lived on the pond, probably in the same broken-down farmhouse they lived in now. Jessie didn't tell Terri that she knew, and she didn't tell her father. Something terrible had happened to Mitch Carr since then. He'd turned mean or gone crazy from his downtrodden life. Jessie thought it would be better for her father to stay away from Mitch, and from the brothers, who didn't sound very reliable. It was safer for all the Kettels to keep away from the Carrs, Jessie decided.

Except for Terri. Terri was great.

Not long after their second visit to the fox kits, Jessie was poling them both down the pond when Terri announced,

"Okay, we're going in to the Cuttings' to look around. I just found out there used to be a workshop there."

"What kind of workshop?"

"What do you think? Tools! I bet you thought I'd forgotten about fixing up this bathtub, but I didn't. I've been working on it."

They brought the waterlogged raft through the reeds to the bank below the big house with the porches, and got off.

Terri said, "We'll have to sneak up from here. Somebody might be looking out the window."

They went through bushes up the left side of the wide lawn, behind a row of bent-over, crook-limbed pine trees. The winter did that to trees along the coast, Jessie's father had told her. Winds could get up to forty or fifty miles an hour, more if there was a storm. That was why there were no tall trees, only bent and stunted ones, even on a grand estate like this.

"Watch out for gardeners," Terri murmured. "They've got a mass of people working on this place. All for one little old lady, imagine that."

Terri said the workshop was supposed to be in the garage and they might be able to get in because the door might be open. Her dad had told her.

"But we don't want to go in, do we?" Jessie whispered. "It's not our property."

"So?" Terri gave her a glance. "Okay. If you want, we'll just look for now. Mitch is usually right about stuff like this, though. He worked for them a while back."

"Here?"

"Yes, for the Cuttings. He said there are a lot of tools in the garage that nobody ever uses. They're just hanging up, rusting."

They tried to look through a window but couldn't see anything. Terri found a door around back, screened by bushes. It wasn't locked. She looked at Jessie, shrugged, and went inside. After a minute Jessie followed. She closed the door behind herself so no one would see they'd gone in.

The garage wasn't for cars anymore. It was a storage place crammed with household junk: old rugs, chairs and tables, cardboard boxes full of stuff wrapped up in yellowed newspaper. A huge Chinese vase painted with a fire-breathing dragon sat in a box of its own. Under the windows a bronze table lamp with a colorful stained-glass shade was pushed against the wall. Layers of dust had sifted down over everything. The floor was so old that the concrete had cracked and sunk in places. They were careful where they walked. The air smelled earthy and damp.

"I don't see any tools," Terri said.

There was a half-hidden alcove built off one side of the room. While Terri investigated a box of old china ("This stuff is beautiful! Somebody should be using it!"), Jessie crossed over and looked inside. It was the workshop, shrouded in cobwebs but all set up, neat as a pin. The tools hung in immaculate order around the walls: hammers small to large; saws in ascending lengths; screwdrivers, drills, and picks flanked above the workbench; glass bottles full of nails sorted by size, from tiny tacks to giant, peglike spikes.

"Terri. Here it is."

She came at once and gave a little gasp. "This is great."

"No one's been in here for ages, you can tell."

A heavy iron rod with a snoutlike end was leaning against a wall. Terri went over and lifted it up for Jessie to see.

"This is a crowbar," she said. "This is what we need."

"Do you think they'll let us borrow it?"

Terri snorted. "Oh sure, they'll let us. They won't even know."

"But I think we should ask first."

Terri said she wouldn't recommend it.

They were beginning to argue about this when a sound came from the driveway. A car was pulling up outside the garage. Jessie ducked with a beating heart. A car door closed and there was the crunch of footsteps crossing the gravel drive.

Terri crept to the window and looked out. She glanced back at Jessie with a smirk.

"No big deal, it's just the deliveryman from Dolan's. He's bringing in some groceries. Sit tight. He'll be gone in a minute."

She was right. He came out a few minutes later, started his engine, and drove off. Even so, Jessie was nervous. She said they should leave immediately in case someone else showed up. Terri didn't want to, but she came away slowly. She couldn't get over all the boxes of things, especially the beautiful china.

"Can you believe the stuff that's just sitting in here?

What a waste!" she whispered. "Somebody could be using it. There's enough here for somebody's whole house!"

"The furniture looks kind of old," Jessie said doubtfully.

"Nothing's wrong with it, though. I bet most of this stuff could be fixed up like new. Look at that vase. It should be in a museum."

They went out of the garage, closed the door, and sneaked down the hill behind the stunted trees. By then the afternoon was winding down. Terri wanted to get back to pick up the mail before Mitch came home. ("There might be a bill or something that'll get him upset. I know how to handle that stuff.") Jessie said she'd drop her off. They took turns poling the raft up to the sand spit in front of the Carrs' house. The whole way Terri was excited, more excited than Jessie had ever seen her.

"So, no problem. We'll pull the raft up there"—the Cuttings' field, she meant—"and work on it. It's real private. Nobody can see us. There's even some big old planks in the garage. I saw them leaning against the wall in the corner. Wow, did we luck into something! My dad was right!"

"I really think it would be better to ask somebody before we borrow anything," Jessie said. "What if someone sees us going in and out?"

"Who's going to see us? The only people who live there are the old lady and the live-in that takes care of her."

"I still think . . ."

Terri lost her patience.

"Listen! You don't know anything about how things work

around here. It's simple: If we ask, they won't let us. They don't care about what we need. They don't care that they forgot these tools are even there. You can't borrow from people like them. Their stuff is their stuff and they would never let you use it. Especially not for free. If we want to fix the raft, we have to do it this way. It's okay, really. Nobody's going to get hurt. We'll put everything back. They won't even know we've been in there or that anything was ever gone. And we'll have a new raft."

EIGHT

They took the crowbar first.

It wasn't easy dragging the raft out of the water. It weighed a ton and stuck in the mud at the edge. Terri cut bunches of tall field grass with her switchblade, and they laid the grass down in front of the raft. They tried pulling it again. The raft slid, inch by inch, up over the grass until it rested in the Cuttings' field.

Terri looked at it and said: "You know what? This big piece that's on the top should be on the bottom. This raft has been upside down all this time. No wonder it wouldn't float right."

They went to work with the crowbar. Terri pried and Jessie pulled. The thick, waterlogged timber creaked and splintered and came up . . . about three inches. They were so tired by then, they couldn't do any more. They left the raft where it was, split up, and went home, muddy but happy.

They worked on it again the next day, and the day after that, gradually peeling away the rotten wood on top. They progressed slowly. Some days they lasted only an hour or two before they lay back, exhausted. Then they'd sit and talk until Terri had to leave to do some job at her house, or Jessie needed to go home to stay with Jonathan while her father ran errands.

Sometimes Terri walked back with Jessie to the Kettels' cottage, just for something to do. She wouldn't stay if Jessie's father appeared in the yard. She shied away from running into him, which was fine with Jessie. But if Terri saw Jonathan out there alone, that was a different story, because Jessie had told her about Jonathan's insects.

"He crawls around with a glass jar, capturing helpless little spiders and crickets. Then he examines them with this magnifying glass Dad bought him," Jessie had said, laughing. "He counts their legs!"

Terri hadn't laughed. She said she used to do that. ("Not with a magnifier. Never had one of those.") She began to keep an eye out around the raft for bugs she thought Jonathan would like. If she found him outside in the afternoons, she'd call him over and show him what she'd caught.

"I thought you might like this one," she'd say in a soft, conspiratorial voice, opening the paper bag she'd kept it in. Jonathan's eyes would light up.

She brought him a giant water bug with enormous pincers that he loved so much he named it. Arthur, for his best friend back home. ("I bet you miss him," Terri said as they hovered over the bug. "I do," Jonathan told her with a sad nod. "I keep wishing he was here.")

Another time she gave him a plastic sandwich bag full of wood-boring beetles with silvery stomachs.

"Don't take them inside," Terri warned. "They could eat your whole house down once they get started. They're in our porch, so I know what I'm talking about."

"Oh, I won't!" Jonathan whispered. "Thanks so much, Terri. I'll be really, really careful!"

Terri never went inside their house either. Even the one time Jessie invited her in when no one was home, Terri shook her head.

"I've got muddy feet," she said. "I don't want to mess anything up. I'll see you tomorrow." She jogged off and was gone, back to the other end of the pond.

Mornings were when they got the most done. Jessie began to feel a real happiness working beside Terri. She was so smart and good with her hands. And determined, no matter what. Even if she smashed her finger with the crowbar, which happened a lot, she never got mad. She'd jump around, whistling and blowing on it, laugh at herself, and get back to work.

"You don't give up, do you?" Jessie said once, so admiringly that Terri turned away and pretended not to hear. But a minute later she offered Jessie half of a peanut butter sandwich she had in her pocket. It looked a little squashed. Jessie said, "No thanks."

"I always carry food. Just in case," Terri said, tucking the sandwich away.

"In case of what?"

"Oh, you know, of what might happen. Like I might get caught somewhere and have to be there for a while. It probably doesn't happen that much to you."

Jessie agreed that it didn't.

When it was time to quit, they'd walk down the shore in opposite directions and wave from a distance.

"You don't have to come all the way to my house tomorrow," Jessie would sometimes call. "I can meet you here."

But the next morning, when Jessie glanced out, Terri would be sitting on the grass in the Kettels' front yard. She'd be wearing her brother's too-big flip-flops and her same cut-off jeans and a blue plaid shirt with the sleeves rolled up. She looked so much the same that sometimes Jessie wondered if she'd slept there.

One morning Jessie's father got up earlier than usual.

"I brought a croissant out to Terri," he said when Jessie came into the kitchen. "We had a nice conversation. She told me she lives down at the end of the pond."

"I guess she does," Jessie said quickly. She was so afraid her father would go out and talk to Terri again, and find out who her family was, that she grabbed a croissant and ran to meet her before anything else could happen.

"You're getting here so early. Nobody's even awake when you come!" she said when they'd walked clear of the yard.

"Is that a problem?"

Jessie didn't want to say it was.

"Your dad came out and talked to me. We had a great conversation," Terri said. "I really like him."

"I know. He told me."

"He kept inviting me in. He seemed pretty cool about everything."

"Well, he isn't always. He can be a real pain," Jessie said sharply.

Terri glanced at her. She stopped walking and made Jessie stop so they could be face-to-face.

"What's the matter? Is something wrong?"

Jessie said there wasn't.

"Can't your dad talk to me if he wants to? Did somebody say something against me?"

Jessie was embarrassed. "No, of course not! Come whenever you want. It's fine, really!"

Terri looked relieved.

"Well, good. I like to come," she said. "I like sitting and watching the sun rise over your house. I like how everyone gets up for breakfast and everything starts, real quiet and easy."

"That's because we're on vacation," Jessie said. "You should see us back home when we have school. My mom is trying to get Jonathan dressed, and my dad is making breakfast and burning the toast, and we're all yelling that we're going to be late. It's a madhouse."

Terri started walking again. "See, to me, that doesn't sound that bad," she said over her shoulder.

They arrived at the raft site that day to find a whirl of activity going on up at the Cutting house. Cars were pulling into the driveway. People were rushing around. A woman in a white coat emerged on the wide porch overlooking the pond and walked from one end to the other. Jessie and Terri crouched down behind the bushes in the field.

Terri whispered, "That's the live-in. She's the main one that takes care of the old lady. Looks like she's on the war-path."

Jessie flattened herself on the ground. The woman's head was turning left and right, spying into corners of the yard.

"Maybe something happened to her," Terri whispered.

"Who?"

"Miss Cutting. Sometimes she gets loose and wanders around here. She's kind of mental now."

"Mental how? Does she have Alzheimer's?"

"Whatever. They keep her locked up most of the time. She could get lost or fall in the pond. She was never quite right in the head since she was a kid. You know, after every-thing that happened. Now it's gotten worse. At least, that's what I heard."

"So tell me again—"

"Not now!" Terri hissed. "Look. There she is!"

Jessie looked up. A shadowy figure was moving toward them through the bushes. Long and thin, it disappeared for a minute behind a mass of green leaves. In the next moment a very old woman appeared several yards away, walking with a halting step.

"Hello?" she called in a trembling voice. She staggered and fell.

Jessie and Terri watched her go down in silence. They

watched her struggle to get back up. She grasped a nearby bush with both hands and pulled herself to her feet with a groan. Her glasses had slid sideways. She reached up to hook one dangling side back behind an ear. With Jessie and Terri once again in view, she smiled.

"There you are! So silly of me. What you must think! An old woman in her dotage. But here I am, nevertheless! Free for a moment. I wanted to come down and speak to you girls. I've been watching you. I know what you're doing."

"We haven't stolen anything—" Terri began.

"Of course not!" Miss Cutting interrupted. "That's what I've come to say. It's all yours. I haven't been out on it since I was a girl, of course. It's in bad shape, I can see. But you must feel free to use it. Yours. I'm delighted. I give my raft to you. There!"

She stretched her hands out toward Terri, who lurched back out of reach. Jessie stepped forward. She clasped hands with Miss Cutting and smiled at her.

"Thank you so much! It's so nice of you to come down and tell us." The old lady's fingers felt like a bundle of dry sticks.

"Not at all. Not at all. I'm only too pleased. I would invite you both up to the house, but . . ."

They turned to look up there. The hustle and bustle was continuing. People were congregated on the porch, walking down the porch steps, fanning out across the lawn in several directions.

"They'll have the dogs out soon!" the old lady said gaily.

"Dogs!" Terri looked truly alarmed.

Henrietta Cutting glanced at her with special interest.

"You live at the end of the pond, don't you? I've seen you from the window. I thought you were one of the Coopers at first, but you don't look like them. That family was red-haired."

Terri took another nervous step back.

"You needn't worry, there aren't any dogs," Miss Cutting assured her. "I only meant that I don't have much time. They'll be looking for me down here if I don't go back. And we can't have that, can we?"

Terri said faintly, "No."

"It's up to you girls to keep our secret down here. And up to me to keep it up there." Miss Cutting leaned forward and lowered her voice. "I'm counting on you both, you know."

"For what?" Jessie asked.

At this moment the chattering on the porch rose to a more frantic pitch and from its midst a single voice shrieked through the air.

"Henrietta! Where are you? I've had enough of this. Come back here at once!"

"That is the bark of my private nurse," Henrietta told the girls. "Stay away from her, whatever you do. She would ruin everything. I will be in touch again soon!"

She turned and stumbled uphill through the bushes. Jessie and Terri lay back down on the ground and watched her go. In a little while they heard the sounds of her arrival at the house. "Goodness, where have you been?" and "We were so worried! You must never go off that way again!"

They saw the old woman being handed up the steps of the porch and taken indoors. The people on the porch went inside after her. A little while later the cars in the driveway began to leave.

"That's so strange, her coming down here," Jessie whispered. "Was this really her raft?"

Terri laughed. "Get real. If she ever had one, it would've rotted years ago. I wouldn't believe anything that lady says. She's crazy as a loon, doesn't hardly know what century she's in."

"Who are the Coopers?"

"That's what I mean. That family was here years ago, before I was even born. They lived where the old chimney is now. A hurricane took out their house and they never came back."

"Well, she seems not to mind us fixing up the raft," Jessie said. "She seems to want us here."

"I wouldn't bet on it," Terri said grimly. "People say things like that all the time. Then they change their minds and call the police."

"I don't think she'd do that."

"Why not?"

"She just seemed really nice."

Terri stared at her. "You don't know," she said. "You don't know how things work. Anyway, I'm not sticking around. Let's give the raft a rest. I've got stuff to do at home."

Jessie nodded. "Sure. What about tomorrow?"

"I don't know yet. Maybe. I'll see how it goes."

Terri jogged off in the direction of her house.

But the next morning she was not waiting outside the Kettels' cottage. She was not at the raft when Jessie tramped over to the Cuttings' field after breakfast. That day, she never came. Jessie hung around for an hour, wondering if Miss Cutting's strange appearance had scared her off for good. She didn't dare go on to the Carrs' house to find out.

She walked slowly home, turning once to glance up at the closed face of the grand house above. If Miss Cutting was watching, there was no way to tell. The doors were shut tight. The windows showed only a pale reflection of the sky. You'd never know that anyone was living inside.

Unless you'd met her, Jessie thought. And what was it that poor, crazy Henrietta Cutting was counting on them to do?

NINE

W hat happened to the Silent Lamb?" Jessie shouted up to Julia.

They were walking along the weedy border of the road, on their way to the beach. Every vehicle that went by sent a hard buffet of wind into their faces.

"What?" shouted Julia, without breaking stride.

"Your preppy boyfriend with the car. What's his name, Aaron something? Where is he?"

"He was not ever my boyfriend!" Julia yelled back. A line of five or six cars passed, making conversation impossible. It was after eleven. Extreme heat was forecast. The sun blazed from a sapphire sky. Without Terri, Jessie was at loose ends. Julia had said she could tag along with her to the beach, if she didn't mind walking.

"So you dumped him already?" Jessie asked during a lull.

Julia didn't answer. She strode ahead under the scrutiny of passing traffic, dark brown hair streaming back in the breeze. Jessie, who disliked being observed by strangers in public places, trailed behind. When her bangs blew up in a gust of wind, she pushed them flat with her hand and held them there.

They had on backpacks stocked with towels, sandwiches, sunblock, and other supplies for the day. Their suits were under their clothes—in Julia's case, a man-size chamois shirt that ended just above her knees, leaving her long, slim legs charmingly on view. She was walking barefoot and gave a little leap from time to time to avoid a rock or piece of road-side glass. At intervals she paused to check her cell phone, which occasionally connected, though never long enough to hold a conversation.

"This is *such a nuisance*!" she said after each stop.

Jessie wore the rubber flip-flops Terri had given her and, embarrassed by the bathing suit her mother had made her buy (big ruffles in front), an army-green waterproof poncho that dropped to midcalf.

"I see treacherous weather on the horizon," her father had teased as she left the house. "A typhoon blowing up from the West Indies."

"Dad, that is so totally rude!"

They reached the beach and chose a place to spread their towels among the crowd of umbrellas. People were lying or sitting everywhere on the sand. The water was packed with swimmers. Out on the rocks children were jumping off diving boards cemented at different levels into the stone. The high dive was especially popular. With every launch, delirious screams of terror echoed inshore.

"I may not be staying here, depending on who I run

into," Julia announced. She took off her chamois shirt and stretched out on her towel in a sinuous, catlike way that, to Jessie, was completely insufferable.

"What is that book you're reading?" Julia asked.

"*Invisible Man*," Jessie said. She pulled off her poncho and sat down. "It's about racism. How some people are so blinded by prejudice they can't see the real person right in front of them," she explained, though her sister's eyes had closed and it was obvious she wasn't really listening. "To them, the real person is completely invisible."

"I can never read on beaches," murmured Julia. This was surprising, since to Jessie's knowledge, she'd never been on a real ocean beach before this trip. It didn't seem safe to challenge her, though. Jessie hunched cross-legged on her towel, squinting down at a page whose print was blanked by the dazzling sun.

"Beaches are such healthful places," Julia continued in an irritating tone. "All human beings, given a choice, feel happiest near large bodies of water. There's something about looking out over water that brings peace to the soul."

Jessie glanced out to sea. Her soul did not feel at peace. What was going on with Terri?

"It's a chemical thing," Julia said, lying perfectly still on her towel while an active beauty blazed forth from her skin. "Our cells respond somehow. We came from the sea, you know. It's like looking at our mother."

"Get real," Jessie said, quoting Terri. "There's someone coming," she added. A male figure in red swim trunks was making his way toward them with decisive steps.

Julia sat up to look and quickly lay back down. She shut her eyes. "Aaron Bostwick. Don't talk to him."

He arrived and stood over them, blocking their sun.

"I thought I was picking you up," he burst out to Julia. "You could have told me, you know."

"Told you what?" Julia asked, breaking her own vow of silence but keeping her eyes closed.

"That you were walking!" Aaron Bostwick's voice rose to a plaintive tenor. "I wasn't even planning to be at the beach today. If I'd known you didn't need a ride, I wouldn't've even bothered to come. There's plenty of other things I could do, you know."

"So go and do them," Julia said. "What's stopping you?"

Aaron's shadow shifted away with a jerk, allowing the sun to blaze down on them. He made a strange noise that sounded like a clogged drain. "What is *that* supposed to mean?"

"I have no idea," Julia said. "You tell me."

A long silence opened up. Jessie lowered her head and glued her eyes to the invisible print of *Invisible Man*.

"Well, do you want me to pick you up anymore or not?" Aaron said finally, shadowing them again. His voice had come down a notch. "At least you should tell me that."

Julia nodded slowly, as if she'd lost track of the conversation, or perhaps was even falling asleep.

"Well, what?" Aaron said. "What do you want?"

Julia shook her head no.

"You know, you could at least *look* at me," Aaron said. "You could at least say something! I can't believe this!"

Julia sighed and sat up. She put on her sunglasses and looked at him. "Is that better?"

This comment caused an eruption that could only be described as volcanic. "You are so bad!" he shouted at her. "You ask me to drive you, and then you don't even wait for me to come. You just kind of forget, or I don't know, as if it's not even important."

"Is it important?" Julia asked, adjusting her sunglasses.

"You're going to be sorry you said that," Aaron Bostwick announced darkly. "You can't just be that way with people. You'll see. You can't!"

He rushed off toward the clubhouse, returning Jessie and Julia to the sun's blaze. Julia lay back on her towel.

"Well, you certainly got *him* worked up," Jessie said. "The Silent Lamb can speak when he wants to."

"He's an idiot. Everybody thinks so."

"He's pretty mad now, that's for sure."

"He'll get over it."

Julia rolled onto her stomach and put a hat over her head. In this position she apparently really did go to sleep, because for an hour or more no sound came from her. Eventually she stirred again and yawned and said: "I'm expecting to meet someone around now, I think."

But then, since no one came, she sat up and ate her sandwich and began to talk about something that actually interested Jessie.

"You know that big house we can see on the pond? It's famous around here because a terrible murder happened there once. Some kids were talking about it. Some maniacs went into the house to rob it and got the owners out of bed. They took them downstairs and shot them. Then they went upstairs to look for their little daughter. She'd seen them commit the murders, I guess. So they hunted and hunted, but in the end they couldn't find her. Then they robbed the house, took jewelry and a lot of other stuff. Afterward the police caught the main killer, but the daughter was too upset to be at the trial. She had to be sent away. Years later she came back and started accusing people around town of being murderers. Like people she ran into, all of a sudden she'd point at them and say 'Murderer!' in a terrible voice. Actually, she's still there in that house. They keep her inside most of the time."

Julia bit into her sandwich thoughtfully and added: "I guess her mind totally slipped over the years. I guess when something like that happens, right before your eyes, you lose all sense of reality."

Jessie said, "Who told you this?"

"Ripley Schute." Julia glanced down the beach. "He should be here any minute. He's going to Princeton in the fall. I met him a couple of days ago, and listen to this: He told me that he was one of the people the old lady pointed at one time and called a murderer. Just out of the blue. 'Murderer!' He said it made his blood go cold as ice."

TEN

"Do you know anything about a murder that happened once in that big house down from us on the pond?" Jessie asked her father that evening.

He shook his head. "Never heard of it."

"How about the Peckham boys? Did you ever hear of them?"

"No."

Dinner was long over. The day's terrific heat had yet to wear off. The Kettels, all four of them, were lying limply on various chairs and couches around their decrepit living room. Most of the lamps were off to save the fuses. From outside came the noises of the pond, a chaotic symphony of buzzes and chirps, rattles and slurps. A sudden, unidentifiable shriek had brought both stories splashing into Jessie's mind.

"Who are the Peckham brothers?" Jonathan asked sleepily.

The Kettels were now more than two weeks into their Rhode Island vacation. They'd grown familiar with the pond sounds. More than that, they'd come to like them, to feel at home with them and with this creaky old cottage and its endless difficulties.

Richard Kettel was sleeping through the night as he hadn't for many months in Pittsburgh. ("It's so uncomplicated here," he said.)

Jonathan still woke in the dark, but hearing the pond through the window, he knew where he was. He'd glance over at Jessie and fall back asleep without bothering anyone.

In their separate rooms, Julia and Jessie let the pond's sound track wash over them while they read or reviewed the day's events and waited for sleep. ("It really is a kind of music. I'm writing a poem about it," Julia said airily.)

"The Peckham *boys*," Jessie corrected Jonathan in the living room. "I think they were cousins. Or maybe they just came from families that had the same name."

"Or maybe they were pecked," Jonathan said.

"What?"

"Peck-ham," Jonathan explained. "Julia's boyfriend looks pecked all over his face."

"That's acne," Jessie said, suppressing a laugh.

Julia did not smile. "When Jonathan grows up, he's going to be one of those pathetic stand-up comics who aren't even funny," she said sourly. She put on her earphones and curled away.

"No, I'm not. I'm going to be a mologist."

"A what?" Jessie asked.

"Entomologist," her father said. "Jonathan and I were talking about it today. The study of insects, right, Jonathan?"

"But first you have to go to college," Jonathan said. "Then you can get in a lab and wear a special coat and do your own speriments. That's what I want to do."

"You have to get through graduate school too," his father said, "which costs a royal fortune. Are you prepared to pay for it yourself?"

"No!" Jonathan said. "That's what you're supposed to do!"

The room fell into silence after this remark, which cut a bit close to the family bone.

Richard Kettel's parents, both teachers, had not been well-off. They weren't as poor as some in their neighborhood, but there was never quite enough for luxuries. Like this seaside vacation, he might have said. Or college. Jessie and Julia knew their father had had to raise a large part of the money to go. Once there, he'd worked his way through, dropping out some semesters to make enough for the next.

Their mother's life had been different. She came from a family that was able to support her, even through law school. She'd inherited a trust fund too and now drew a hefty income from her law firm, much more than their father's high school teaching brought in.

The result was that money was a touchy subject in the Kettel house. There was plenty to go around; the issue lay elsewhere. Their mother spent freely and comfortably for whatever the family needed: clothing, electronics, bedroom furniture, new books. Their father, from long habit, questioned every item and dug in his heels. "Need" was a slippery slope to him.

"*What's wrong with the library?*" he'd ask. "*Money doesn't grow on trees,*" he'd growl. "*Waste not, want not,*" he repeated endlessly. "*A fool and his money are soon parted,*" he warned them all.

In the living room Julia and Jessie tensed, ready to hear him spout off to Jonathan on this score. But tonight he let it pass. Maybe Jonathan was still too young to get the full treatment.

"A lot of people are related in this town," he said instead, changing the subject. "The old farms are mostly gone, but some descendants of the big families that used to run them have stuck around, gone into other lines of work. You can still see family resemblances if you look. Among the locals, I mean. Noses, cheekbones, hair color. Rugged New England looks from way back. Gives you a real sense of place."

"If you ask me, the summer people are the ones who look alike," Jessie said. "Everybody's wearing dark glasses and polo shirts and driving around in SUVs."

This was actually something Terri had said.

"Good point." Her father nodded. "We must look like outsiders to them."

"We're more than outsiders. We're clueless," Jessie said. "We don't know anything about what's really going on in this town. There's a whole level of stuff we never hear about."

"Well, I've heard about the Peckham boys." Julia had taken off her earphones to be part of the conversation. "Didn't they drown or something?"

"In this pond, a long time ago." Jessie looked out the

window into the dark, toward where the pond would be if she could see it "They got sucked down in quicksand and were never found. Terri says they've been haunting the place ever since. That's just a story, of course. I think the boys were real."

"Oh, Terri!" Julia turned on Jessie in disgust. "Why are you even bothering with her? She comes from a terrible family."

"Who said that?"

"Rip told me."

"Who?"

"Ripley Schute. He said her father is a drunk who can't hold down a job and her mother isn't even there anymore. She left. There are a couple of brothers who got arrested for burning down a barn. Their house is at the end of the pond, and the police are always over there for something. Rip said it's a total dump. They don't even have decent plumbing."

Jessie sat up. "So? What does that have to do with Terri? You're such a snob, Julia. You don't even know her."

"I've seen her."

"Well?"

"Well, she looks creepy. I hate the way she sits outside our house in the morning. I bet she's planning to steal something. Rip said it was a member of their family that murdered the people in that big house, in a robbery. A great-grandfather or something. He spent his whole life in prison. You should watch out, Jessie. Terri's not like us at all."

"You should watch what you say about people you don't

know. In fact, you should just shut up," Jessie said. Except she didn't say it, she screamed it.

"Hey, Jessie, cool down." Her father put his hand on her arm. "Julia, that's pretty nasty. Terri seems like a perfectly nice person. I've talked to her. She and Jessie are just cruising around the pond on a raft they found. I think that's great."

"I found," Jessie said. "My raft."

"Sure."

"I invited Terri to be on it. It's waterlogged, though. Terri knows the right tools we need to fix it."

Her father looked at her.

Jonathan, who had dozed off, came suddenly awake. "A raft? Can I go on it?"

"No."

"Why not?"

"It's private. And we're still working on it."

"Where?" her father asked. "Where are you working on it? At Terri's house?"

"No."

He looked as if he didn't believe her. "Because it sounds like you might want to steer clear of Terri's house. It sounds like her family is a little . . . well, that there are some problems. You aren't fixing the raft over there, are you, Jessie?"

"No!"

"Where are you working on it, then?"

With this, Jessie boiled over. "What is this, the Spanish Inquisition?" she yelled. "You all have a really bad attitude.

Terri and I are fixing up the raft, and she's great. She's amazing. Wherever we're doing it, it's none of your business."

A long silence took over in the living room, a much worse silence than the one about money. After a while her father carried the sleeping Jonathan up to bed and retired to his own room without saying good night. A little later Julia headed upstairs to her room and closed the door. Jessie sat rigid on the couch.

An unsettled feeling had entered the Kettel household, something ugly and shadowy. Outside the windows the pond was whooping it up with birdish cries and froggy croaks. Late at night was when the pond came most alive, Jessie knew. In deep darkness it dropped the innocent tweets and poetic murmurs of evening and opened up with its real voice, the predatory gulping, swallowing, throttling sounds of the raw, natural world. Listening to them now, Jessie heard a kind of savagery out there that rose to a new level. She was glad she had the four walls of their cottage around her.

An hour went by. Gradually the noise altered, softened, became a low, monotonous drone announcing the onset of a deeper region of night. Even Jessie, sitting tense and angry on the couch, was soothed. Finally she yawned, gave in, and went upstairs to brush her teeth and crawl into bed, where she fell asleep with impressive ease, considering the violent wave of fury that had just passed through her.

ELEVEN

Terri was waiting outside when Jessie checked early the next morning. She was sitting in the same place as usual but hunched over, as if she was looking for something in the grass. Jessie got out there fast.

"Hey. Are you okay?"

Terri nodded without looking up.

Jessie said, "I'm really glad you're here. My dad got jelly doughnuts for breakfast. Want one? Nobody else is up. I'll go get a couple and be right back."

Something was wrong with Terri. Before Jessie asked what, she wanted to get her away from the house. She didn't want her father to come out and talk to Terri again, and she especially didn't want Julia to see her. Terri had a mark the color of Jonathan's blueberry tongue on one side of her face. She turned away and tried to hide it when Jessie came back with the doughnuts.

"How long have you been out here?"

"Not that long," Terri said. Her lips were swollen.

They walked in silence all the way to the Cuttings' field.

The raft was there just the way they'd left it. But the crowbar was in a different place. It was leaned neatly up against a rock over to one side.

"Somebody's been here," Terri exclaimed. "Somebody's been poking around."

"Might've been Miss Cutting," Jessie said. "She might've come down to see us again."

"You think?" Terri looked up toward the house.

"She's the only one who knows we're here."

"I guess." Terri stared suspiciously at the house, then shrugged. "I guess if she was going to turn us in, she would've done it by now."

"So where were you yesterday?" Jessie asked. "Why didn't you come?"

Terri laughed sarcastically. "It's pretty obvious, isn't it? I got clobbered. Don't worry about it. I'm just a little sore right now."

"Did Mitch do it?"

"Yeah, but it was my fault. I should've known to stay out of his way. Don't even think about it, okay? Stuff like this happens at my house. Everybody's used to it. When I go home tonight, he'll be fine again. I cleared out early this morning so he wouldn't have to see."

"See what?" Jessie didn't understand.

"You know, what he did. He feels so bad afterwards. And he has to be at work today."

They sat quietly and ate the doughnuts, Terri chewing as best she could. The sun was coming across the field, lighting everything up. The pond lay in front of them, a cool mirror of the early-morning sky. Terri sat half-turned away from Jessie so that only the good side of her face showed.

"You won't tell anyone, will you?" She cupped her hand over the bruise. "Because I'm okay, really. It's already better today. And because of this raft." She brightened. "I can fix it, I know! Then we can go all over this pond. There's an old dam up at the far end, and a beautiful little pool that's fed by a spring. Indians used to go there to drink. It was their well. When you're there, you can feel them still around, like before the English came and took their land. It's like they're watching from the shadows, and you feel sad for them."

She went on. "We can go and look at that stone chimney where the Coopers' house was. You know what my dad told me once? When the Coopers came back after the hurricane to see what happened, they had the shock of their lives. The whole place was gone, smashed into the pond, except for one teacup sitting up on a rock. One fragile little teacup, balanced there, all alone. The water had gone down and left it there, I guess. I can't believe it, can you? I can't believe it survived."

They took the crowbar up to the Cuttings' workshop and exchanged it for a hammer and a saw. No one was around, which seemed a good sign. The garage was still hot inside from the high temperatures of the day before. The air had a scorched smell, unpleasant to breathe. Terri pocketed some long nails and wiped off her forehead.

"Whew. It must be over a hundred in here."

When she saw a beam of sunlight from outside sparking off an old hand mirror that had come unwrapped from its newspaper covering, she went over and quickly wrapped the mirror back up.

"That's how fires start," she told Jessie. "All this stuff in here, all this furniture, could go up in a flash. I've seen it happen. My great-grandfather's barn was the biggest one in town, and it all burned down to nothing. An old kerosene lamp caused it. The glass heated up in the sun and sparked some hay."

"Your family owned a barn?"

"Down the road a little. We didn't own it when it burned. We'd already had to sell out. The Carr family was big around here at one time. We were in the dairy business and owned land all over town. We owned the land around this pond."

"Why did you have to sell it?"

"Some bad stuff happened that started things going down for us."

"Like what?"

"Well . . ." Terri licked her swollen lips. She dabbed at her lower lip with a finger. The bruise on her face had turned a bright cherry color in the heat. "I'll tell you sometime. Let's get out of here now. I'm sweating like a pig."

They took the tools and also three thick planks of wood that were leaning up against the wall by the door.

"These babies are just begging to come with us," Terri said. She stopped and looked at them again. "Hey, they weren't here before. They were over in that corner."

"They were?"

"Yeah, remember how I told you about them? Someone has been in here! They unwrapped that hand mirror too. It wasn't that way before."

"Must've been her. Miss Cutting," Jessie said. "Who else would come in here? She was looking at her stuff."

This time Terri took longer to convince. All the way back down the hill she worried out loud.

"I don't know about this. Was it really her? Even if it was, who knows what she might do! She scared the liver out of me when she came out of the bushes at the pond. She's totally mental. She could be calling the cops on us right now."

Jessie kept assuring her and shaking her head.

"Terri, I think it's okay. Really, I do. You know, I've been thinking about her a lot. She might be crazy some of the time, but she wants something from us. That's why she came down to see us in the first place. I think she was out yesterday trying to find us again."

It hadn't been easy getting away from the house the second time, but Henrietta managed to accomplish it by midafternoon. Sally Parks was off for the day. Her replacement was a timid girl from the agency who didn't know the first thing about what she was supposed to do.

"Are you sure you're allowed downstairs? No one said you did that. Walked around here, I mean. Well, okay, if you think it's all right."

She edged Henrietta at a snail's pace down the front staircase, over the worn places in the carpet, into the dingy, plantless solarium. The house was not so well kept as it had once been. Henrietta seated herself in a sagging padded chair.

"Are you all right there, Mrs. Cutting?"

"Miss Cutting," Henrietta corrected her. "I never married."

"Oh! Sorry! They didn't tell me. Well, are you okay by yourself for a while?"

Henrietta nodded. She drooped her head against the cushion to indicate that a nap was probably not far off.

"I shall be fine here for quite some time," she said with a fake tremble in her voice. Overdramatic, but it worked.

The incompetent replacement went off to the kitchen to talk to someone on the telephone. Henrietta's hearing had stayed reliable, even in these latter years. From the kitchen pantry she heard:

"Yeah, no problem. She's out cold. The poor thing can hardly walk. It took us about an hour to come downstairs. I hope I never get that way."

So, up, up, and away. Five minutes later Henrietta was out the solarium door and around the side of the house. She headed downhill to the raft first, hopeful that the girls would be there again. But they were not. A crowbar was lying askew between muddy tufts of grass. Her father, ever careful of his tools, would never have stood for such a thing! She picked up the crowbar and leaned it against a nearby rock, out of the damp. Then she headed uphill to the garage, puffing with anticipation.

She'd seen the girls coming and going from there through her binoculars. Now (the crowbar!) she understood. Very exciting! They were using her father's tools, bringing them down to the raft. They were starting to fix it, just as she'd been telling them to do.

It was really marvelous how they'd taken up the burden of this project. "We are *in communication*," Henrietta would tell them when she found them in the garage. They were wonderful girls, young and full of independence, as she had been herself at that age. The pond girl with the messy black hair was the leader. She knew what she wanted and how to take it. The other, usually trailing behind, was having an adventure. She looked a little out of her element.

In her excitement Henrietta had trouble with the door into the garage. It wouldn't open. She used both hands on the knob, put her shoulder against it, and finally got in with a mighty push and a cry. A rush of hot air hit her face. The place was a furnace inside.

The girls weren't immediately visible. Despite the heat, Henrietta made her way across the garage (what were all these boxes doing here?) to the alcove at the back. She gazed hopefully into her father's workshop. No girls. But his tools were there, lined up in their familiar places, on their familiar hooks: the wrenches and saws, hammers and screwdrivers, wedges and picks.

She entered, brushing aside cobwebs, and went over to

the workbench, a dusty wooden shelf that ran the length of the alcove. She picked up a block plane, examined it, and put it down. She ran her hands over the cast-iron vise secured by screws to the workbench edge. She manipulated its head and spindle with a practiced motion. The vise obediently opened. And closed. Amazing how familiar it felt after all these years.

She must take up woodworking again! She could build things. Time hadn't changed her a bit. She remembered everything, felt the hammer in her hand even now, and that curious sense of mastery that came with the making of things. She wanted to make things again! She could start over from where she left off as a child, relive her life, follow a different route that would take her . . . where? Holding on to the edge of the workbench, she considered.

And came upon an answer. That would take her home.

Home. A wooziness drifts over her, a shadow on the brain. All at once she is struck by a certainty: *My father is nearby!*

He is here in the garage. Just out of sight. Moving toward her.

She hears his voice.

"Henny! We've got work to do. So much to do and so little time! Your mother expects us for lunch at one o'clock on the dot. We mustn't lose track of ourselves."

Henrietta flings herself around to greet him. For an instant she sees him in the workshop door: broad, full-bodied, handsome in a work shirt and tie, sleeves rolled up and ready to start. They are going to retimber the raft! Several planks have become waterlogged over the winter, and he knows what to do. She does too, actually. He's taught her.

"Oh, Father!" Henrietta cries joyfully. She reaches out. At this moment the room spins, swirls, and collapses around her. She loses sight of him, calls "Father" again, and falls. She slumps to the floor; the workshop dims and fades away.

Minutes later, or was it hours? She's being helped to her feet. Not by her father. It was the agency girl. How had she come to be here?

"Leave me alone," Henrietta snapped. "I can get up by myself."

The girl assisted anyway, putting her hands in the wrong places, nearly tipping her over backward. "You are no help at all!" Henrietta said, pushing her off. The girl stood back in dismay. All this was her fault and she knew it. She should have kept better watch over the old lady.

"Mrs. Cutting, we should go back to the house. You shouldn't be here. If anyone found out . . ." She trailed off.

"Of course I should be here," Henrietta announced, suddenly clear of head, back in the present. "I came to get something. Now, what was it?"

She looked around at the cardboard boxes, the old furniture, the fire dragon vase. Everything was faintly familiar, but she couldn't quite place it.

"It must be here somewhere," she said, pawing into a box, taking things out, playing for time while she tried to think. She picked up an object wrapped in newspaper and unwrapped it. Part of her mind was still in shock, still looking around for her father. Was he in the corner?

The object turned out to be an ivory-handled mirror from a long-ago dressing table. Had it been hers? She held it up, looked, caught sight of ghastly eyes peering back. Who on earth was that? She tossed the mirror away.

"Oh yes, now I remember! Lumber!"

"Lumber?"

Henrietta's glance had fallen on several planks of lumber leaning against the wall in the corner.

"Will you please help me move these boards toward the door?" she asked the girl. "They must be left just inside. Someone will be coming soon to get them. That's it. Thank you so much. We've accomplished what we came to do."

The incompetent said hopefully, "Can I take you back to the house now?"

"Yes, you may." Henrietta glanced at her. "And there's no need to say a word about this, is there?"

"About being here, you mean?"

"That's what I mean. Are we agreed? Not a word."

"Oh, yes!" the girl said. "Not a word. I promise!"

Never had anybody looked so relieved as she suddenly did.

TWELVE

Six days later, in the field below the Cuttings' house, Jessie stepped back and surveyed the raft with a critical eye.

"I hope we aren't making it worse," she said. "I hope it will still float."

"It will. I know what I'm doing," Terri said, hammer in hand. With a strong blow she flattened a protruding nailhead. She was showing off, but that was okay. She deserved to, Jessie thought.

"Where did you learn how to build things?"

"Oh, I've been doing it from way back. Mitch showed me first. We made the henhouses in our yard when I was a kid. Real cute. We gave them little window boxes and shutters. He was a good carpenter at one time."

"But not anymore?"

"Lost interest, I guess. After my mom died." Terri walked around to the other side of the raft and whacked at something else.

"Sorry. I didn't know your mother died. I thought she just kind of . . . left."

"Why would you think that?"

"I don't know."

Terri gave her a sharp glance. "She had a weak heart. It got her in the end. In case you want to spread the word."

"I don't."

"You should watch out for stuff like that," Terri said. "People make things up when they don't know. Whoever you've been talking to, they've got the wrong idea about us. My mom was a great person. She went through some bad stuff in her life, but she never gave up. We really loved her and she really loved us. She wouldn't ever just leave!"

"Oh, Terri, I'm sorry! That was so stupid!"

"It's okay. I know you're basically on my side."

"I am. You must miss her all the time. How old were you when she . . ."

Terri held up her hand.

"Hey, I don't want to talk about it, okay? I got over it. We all got over it. Sometimes the only thing you can do is just get over stuff."

She turned her attention back to the raft. "What do you think? Is this old tub ready to launch?"

It looked ready. Long hours of hard labor had brought them to this point, including so much coming and going from the workshop up the hill that a path had been worn behind the stunted pine trees along the side of the Cuttings' field. The raft seemed more or less repaired. The waterlogged plank had been pried off, and three new ones nailed in its place. This improvement was not visible now because the raft had been turned over.

"How did we even do that?" Jessie had said afterward.

"Stick with me and anything's possible," Terri had boasted. "I'm not the dope some people think."

"Who would ever think that?"

"Some people. They judge you. Do I care? Nope."

Rebuilding the raft had brought out the best in her. All week she'd been in high spirits. The terrible bruise on her face was healing without any special treatment. Just a splash of pond water now and then to cool it down. Jessie had brought a tube of first-aid cream from home, and some sterile pads and tape, but Terri had refused them. When Jessie insisted and warned about infection, Terri blew up.

"Leave me alone! I'm fine! Quit bothering about me," she yelled straight into Jessie's face, which might have hurt Jessie's feelings if she hadn't known already about the one really raw nerve in her friend, the sore spot that no one was allowed to touch. Terri couldn't stand anybody feeling sorry for her. She couldn't stand one ounce of it.

The raft's underside had revealed a thick growth of green slime. They'd cleaned it off with a big sponge from the garage. Next came Terri's idea to build low benches on the raft.

"So we don't need to be standing all the time. And it'll keep our butts dry if some water slops up."

This project, even with the help of a larger saw and more lumber from the garage, had turned out to be beyond them. In the end the benches collapsed and had to be torn off. Terri was not ready to give up even on this. She had another plan for building them again, but Jessie persuaded her to hold off. Maybe later, she said. Time was slipping away. They needed to get the raft back out on the pond.

They'd met early in the morning for the grand launch. At first the raft wouldn't budge from the bank no matter how hard they pulled and pushed. Terri's long-grass solution, which had worked so well getting the raft out of the pond, was no help. The raft had dried out. It wasn't slippery enough.

This time it was Jessie who had the brainstorm.

"How about digging a trench and sluicing it down with mud?"

Terri nodded. "There are some shovels in the garage."

Jessie said she would get them. She'd long ago forgotten to be nervous up there. They'd borrowed quite a number of tools by now, and not always bothered to return them. Hammers, saws, screwdrivers, a hand drill, measures, and nails lay around on the soft ground near the raft, along with discarded ends of wood. They'd take the tools back sometime and hang everything in its proper place. Just not now, when they were so close to finishing. And anyway, they had permission from Miss Cutting, didn't they? Jessie thought so. The old woman knew what they were doing. She'd even encouraged it.

"I'm counting on you. . . . I will be in touch again soon," she'd told them. From time to time Jessie looked up at the windows of the great house. Though no sign came back, she thought Miss Cutting must be watching.

Jessie stepped through the garage door to find the place in a shocking state of disorder. Someone had been in there rummaging around. Everything was unwrapped, and newspaper was strewn about. Some of the cardboard boxes had been emptied; some were gone completely. The Chinese vase was missing. The bronze table lamp with the stained-glass shade had been dragged closer to the door. Perhaps Miss Cutting or her nurse had decided to take some of the more valuable things inside, though if this was true, they'd made a terrible mess of it. Jessie located two rusty shovels leaning up against the wall and walked fast down the hill to report the situation.

"Terri, everything's messed up in the garage!"

"Messed up how?"

"Somebody's been through it since we were there. It looks like they're taking things out."

Terri's face stiffened. "What are they taking?"

"Some boxes are empty that were full of stuff before. Things have been unwrapped and there's newspaper all around."

"Is the pretty china still there?"

"I couldn't see. There's such a mess. That big lamp was near the door, like someone meant to drag it out."

Terri licked her lips. She walked over and took the shovels from Jessie's hands. She stuck them, one after another, in the ground.

"Well, I guess those folks up there finally came to their senses," she said. "There was way too much stuff in that garage. Like I told you, it's a fire hazard to pile things up like that. I'm glad they're finally doing something about it."

"I guess they are," Jessie said, "except it seems like somebody else might've been in there. You should come up and see. I even wonder if somebody broke in."

"Why would they do that?"

"I don't know, but it sure looks like it."

Terri exhaled sharply. "Hey, Jessie. I wouldn't worry about it, okay?"

"What do you mean?"

"I mean don't worry about it. It's out of our hands."

"You mean— "

"It's not our business. And we shouldn't go up there again either."

"But we need to bring the tools back! Especially now, before anyone knows. Otherwise, it will look as if . . ."

Jessie stopped. Terri was shaking her head. She was shaking it so hard that her stringy black hair flew out from the sides.

"Especially *now* is when we shouldn't bring them back, okay? We need to wait."

"Until when?"

"Until whatever is going on up there is done. We don't want to run into anybody, right? We're not part of that scene."

"I guess not."

"No, we aren't," Terri said. She handed Jessie a shovel. "Now let's launch this raft and get out of here."

They went to work digging a channel, broad and shallow, from the raft to the pond. The water level in the ground was high enough that the channel turned slick almost at once. They splashed more water from the pond on top to really sluice it down, then dug in their heels and pushed with all their might. Inch by inch the wooden platform moved. Foot by foot they worked it to the edge. From there they gave it one last mighty shove and forced it into the water.

There were five breathless seconds as the raft's front edge plowed underwater and seemed to wrestle with the pond to rise back up. Then the structure quivered and rose to the surface like an unruly animal coming up for air. Suddenly the whole of it was floating high and light before their eyes.

"Hooray," Jessie breathed.

"Not yet," Terri said. "We still have to test if it'll take us."

She squelched across the mud channel to the raft and pulled herself up on it.

"Steady as the Rock of Gibraltar!" she called back.

So Jessie waded out, carrying the poling stick over her head. Halfway there she slipped and went down, losing one of Terri's flip-flops. It shot away, out of reach.

"Forget it!" Terri called, so she went on without it, reached the raft, and hauled herself aboard. The platform wobbled and creaked with the addition of her weight, then nimbly regained its balance. Both girls were so delighted that for a moment they stood grinning at each other while the raft rocked beneath them, sending ripples in all directions.

"Okay, it floats. Let's get going," Terri commanded.

With a shove they set off from shore, leaving behind their repair site, its scatter of tools and muddy, trampled grass. Jessie looked back once and quickly turned away.

That morning they kept going and going along the reedy fringe of the pond, keeping out of sight as much as possible and not talking. They went until they were so far away from the Cuttings' field that it folded into invisibility, and the house fell behind and was hidden too. Finally Terri threw down the poling stick and said, "Okay, we're safe."

Jessie didn't need to ask "From what?" Her heart had been pounding the whole time. Instead she said, "Let's go swimming."

They went in in their clothes, which were heavy with mud. When they'd washed off, they climbed aboard the raft and lay in the sun to dry off. Around them the pond became peaceful. The cattails murmured and swished in perfect unconcern, as if to prove they were not only safe but lost to the outside world, and that they would keep on being lost until they wanted to be found.

"This is so great," Terri whispered at last.

"I know."

"We could bring some pillows and sleep out here."

"I guess."

"We could live on this thing!"

"We'd need a ton of bug spray to do that."

"We could bring food and soda. We could keep the soda cool by storing it underwater in a net. I have a crab net."

"Are there crabs in this pond?"

"A few. Used to be more. Blue crabs. Used to be more of everything here. Clams, quahogs, eels. Mitch ate out of this pond when he was a little kid. That's how his family got through. There was trout in here back then. He went fishing all the time."

Jessie was tempted to say "I know. My dad was out here with him. They worked together and were friends. My dad remembers how your dad used to be."

In another minute she might have spoken. It seemed they'd reached a place where it was only right to own up to the past, a place where they could show their whole selves and not, as Terri said, be judged for it.

But Terri spoke sooner, and what she said returned the conversation to the world they'd just escaped.

"It's my fault."

"What is?"

"The mess in the garage. I told Mitch about the china and the other stuff there. I should've known. He can't keep his mouth shut. Somebody heard about it and they're in there now."

"Who is?"

"Not Mitch. I don't think he'd do that. Might be one of my brothers. I never know with them. Or somebody else. A lot of people are broke around here. We're not the only ones. Also, there are the druggies. They steal from their own mothers when they have to."

Jessie said, "There are addicts around here? I thought they were only in the cities."

"They're here worse than the cities. But you can't see them because they're inside families. And families cover up.

"So anyway." Terri sat forward. "From now on we can't go to the Cuttings' anymore. We have to leave the tools where they are. The whole place is too hot."

"Hot?" A sick feeling had arrived in Jessie's stomach.

"Dangerous. If it's druggies, we could even get hurt."

"What will happen now?"

"Well, eventually somebody from the house will go in there. Then they'll call the police, who'll come over and investigate. They'll look for footprints and try to trace where the stuff went. They'll probably see our trail going down to the pond."

Jessie's hand rose over her mouth. "They'll find the tools and think it was us."

"Not necessarily. They might think the tools are connected to the break-in, like maybe somebody came in on a boat."

"But what if they ask around and find out we've been there fixing the raft? My dad knows we were doing it. So do Julia and Jonathan. They don't know where, but they know."

"Everyone in my family knows too," Terri said. "But families don't tell on each other, remember? At least mine doesn't. Does yours?"

"I don't know," Jessie said. "I've never had anything happen like this."

"Well, I guess you'll find out."

Jessie swallowed. "I don't think they'd tell on me. Even Julia."

"So don't worry," Terri said.

"What about Miss Cutting? She knows everything!"

Terri sighed. "Even if she talked, who would believe her? Everyone around here knows she's nuts. Look, we just have to hope nobody goes in the garage for a while. A couple of months from now they won't be able to see our path so well."

"By then I'll be home in Pittsburgh!"

"Right," Terri said. "But I'll still be here."

The good feeling had gone out of the day. They didn't want to stay hidden, but neither could they decide where to go next or what to do. Lunchtime was long past. Terri had eaten everything in her pockets for breakfast.

"Hey, I'm starving," she announced. "Let's go back to my place and make sandwiches. We can bring them out here and eat on the raft. It would really be fun."

Jessie shook her head no.

"Nobody's at my house, if that's what's worrying you. Everybody's at work."

"That's okay. I'd rather not."

"Why?"

"I just don't want to."

Terri folded her arms. "There's nothing wrong with my house."

"I know," Jessie said. "I just don't want to go there right now. In fact, I think I want to go home."

"Oh, I get it. Now you're scared to hang out with me."

"No, I'm not."

"Yes, you are. You're scared somebody will find out about us, and you want to go home and hide."

"I do not!" Jessie said angrily.

"Well, then what's the problem?"

"I just don't want to be at your house, okay? Why should I when your dad is crazy and the whole place is a mess and you don't even have plumbing?"

"What?"

Jessie knew instantly that she'd gone too far. The words had come with no warning, from some well-guarded place she'd hardly known was there. Too late, she backpedaled.

"Sorry, Terri. I didn't mean it."

"We have plumbing. Who said we didn't?"

"I don't know. Somebody at the beach."

A hot flush crept across Terri's cheeks. "Who?"

"Some kids. Friends of Julia's. I don't remember their names." She didn't want to say it was Julia.

"I thought you weren't going to hang out with them. I thought you were on my side."

"I wasn't hanging out with them," Jessie protested. "I went to the beach with Julia that day when you didn't come. I read my book there."

"And heard what?"

"Nothing!"

"Yes, you did. You heard about my family. You heard my mother left or something. You heard Mitch was crazy."

"I heard he gets drunk. He does, doesn't he? That's why he goes after you. That's why he feels so bad about it afterwards."

They faced each other on the raft.

"What else?" Terri said. "What else did you hear?"

"Terri, don't."

"Come on. I'd really like to know. What are they saying these days about the no-good Carrs? That we have bad plumbing and stink, that's a new one. What about the barn?"

"What barn?"

"You know what barn." She punched Jessie's arm.

"Ow! That hurt!"

"So tell me."

"Okay! They're saying your brothers burned it down. It wasn't a spark from a kerosene lantern."

"Right. You are certainly talking to the right people. What else?"

Jessie paused. She didn't want to tell the next thing. It seemed shameful even to bring it up.

"Come on!" Terri jeered. "You can do it if you try. Let's hear the whole story! Or maybe you're too nice."

"No, I'm not!"

"Well, let's hear it, then."

"Okay! I heard the murderer was someone in your family."

"Oh, wow. A murderer in my family!"

"I heard he was one of the robbers that killed the husband and wife. He was the man who got sent to prison for life, like you said. That's why you know all about it. That's why you told me that story. Except you never said he was related to you, only that he didn't do it, because you knew I might think—"

Terri shoved Jessie. She shoved her so hard that Jessie fell on the raft and almost went in the water. Terri grabbed the stick and began to pole with furious jabs down the pond. As they went, she talked in bitter spurts of words.

"So they got to you, too. It's always the same. We can't do anything around here without somebody bringing up that murder, without somebody saying how it was the Carrs that did it. Who else would it be? Nobody! Always us."

"If it wasn't you, who was it?" Jessie asked angrily. Terri's shove had made a gash in her knee.

"We got framed."

"Oh, really."

"My dad's grandfather wasn't even there. He got set up. They put all the stolen stuff from the Cuttings' on our dock to make it look like he did it. Somebody called the police and said to look on Eddie Carr's dock."

Jessie's knee had begun to bleed. She tried to stop the blood with her hand, but it gushed through her fingers.

"See, the murder was a contract job," Terri went on.

"I'm bleeding," Jessie said. "Could you hurry up and get me home?"

"I am!" Terri exclaimed. "But first you have to listen. It had nothing to do with us. All we ever did was deliver milk to the Cuttings. Mr. Cutting owned the newspaper in Providence, and somebody wanted to get revenge. They didn't like what the newspaper was writing about them or their business. These guys came up the pond at night, on purpose. They didn't come by the road. My dad's dad told him, and my dad told us. Everybody in my family knows. Eddie Carr got set up from the very beginning."

"Who is Eddie Carr?" Jessie asked, wiping at her knee.

"He's the guy they framed!" Terri screamed at her. "Aren't you even listening?"

Jessie turned her back and stood on the far edge of the raft. She leaned over and splashed some water on her knee. Behind her, Terri stopped poling. When Jessie looked around, she saw her wiping her eyes, which were red and puffy.

"I'm sorry I pushed you."

"It's okay."

"But I need to tell you what really happened."

"Go ahead!"

Terri wiped her eyes and went on.

"After Eddie got sent to the penitentiary, our name and our family got dragged through the mud. People turned against us. Even if they didn't believe Eddie would do that, they didn't buy our milk anymore. They didn't want us delivering to their houses. The dairy went bust. Then my dad's father left. He just left and never wrote and never came back. Then my grandmother couldn't handle things and went off the deep end. People thought we were all crazy. They began to make things up about us that weren't even true. Like that barn that burned down? People say it was the Carrs that burned it. For spite. But why would we do that? We loved that old barn even if we had to sell it to somebody else.

"And now it's worse. Like one time I was buying stuff and

got hauled in for shoplifting. Handcuffs, everything, when I just forgot to pay. And another time I got in a fight with this girl who insulted me, and they said I had a knife and was trying to kill her. And I never even took it out of my pocket. They found it afterwards when I went to the office.

"This knife right here." Terri pulled it out and popped the blade. She waved it at Jessie.

"It's only for protection, which I need in this place, let me tell you. But nobody believed me. I had to go before a judge, and they gave me probation. Then the school kicked me out for a week. Just try coming back after that. Everybody looks at you. They run out of the bathroom when you come in."

Jessie stood as far away from Terri as possible on the raft. She tried to say something but nothing came.

"So that's the real story you won't hear on the beach," Terri said. She popped the blade back in and put the knife in her pocket. She started poling again.

"Not that anyone cares. They don't. Whatever happened in the past is history to them. They're just sitting around waiting for us to screw up again. They want to keep us down, that's part of the deal. When people have you like that, they want to keep it that way. They don't want you ever to come back up."

They reached the landing near the Kettels' cottage. Jessie jumped off and began to walk fast toward her house. Terri's knife had scared her. But there was something worse. It was something Jessie had known all along but had pushed to the side because it seemed so unfair. She saw how Terri was part of it, the whole terrible life the Carrs lived at the end of the pond. There was no keeping her separate. Whatever she did and whatever she said, she was in up to her neck. And if Jessie wasn't careful, she'd get dragged in too.

"Don't go yet!" Terri yelled. "I've got more. A whole lot more. You should know how things really are around here!"

Jessie walked faster. "That's okay. I have to go home now. You keep the raft. It'll be yours anyway in the end."

"What end?" Terri cried. "What are you talking about?"

"I mean when we leave," Jessie answered without looking back. "I mean when this vacation is over, and we leave."

THIRTEEN

During the whole week after her visit to the garage, Henrietta watched for the girls out the window.

She saw them arrive every morning and leave every afternoon. She saw them come up the hill to the garage, disappear inside it, reappear a few minutes later, and run back down the hill. They were taking her father's tools down to the raft to fix it. They took the planks she'd left for them by the door. They had to make three trips because they were so heavy.

She couldn't see the raft itself or the work that was going on. Bushes and trees blocked her view. She would've liked to see. She wanted to be down there helping out, or better yet, doing it herself. She was tempted to make another trip down but held back. If she went too often, Sally Parks might catch her. Then the girls would be discovered. Their secret project would be shut down, along with Henrietta's grand plan: her plot to join them. On the raft. To be back on the pond, where she'd left off all those years ago.

"My goodness, you'd think the World Series was being

played out this window, the way you're at it morning and afternoon," Sally said one day, bringing in lunch on a tray. "What's going on out there—if I may ask?"

"You may not," Henrietta snapped.

"Swans and a flock of geese are all I see," Sally said, pausing behind her.

Henrietta chose this moment to knock over her glass of milk, artfully distracting Sally from noticing the pond girl, who was just exiting the back door of the garage with a large hand drill.

"Oh! So sorry!" Henrietta exclaimed. "Could you run and get a towel to mop up? And I'll need to change my skirt."

One morning it seemed that a problem had developed with the raft, because the pond girl's friend suddenly appeared by herself at the garage. She was covered with mud. She went inside. When she came out, she was carrying two shovels. Shovels!

Henrietta sat forward and focused her binoculars in excitement. She knew what was happening. The repair work was done! The girls were trying to launch the raft. She knew this because long ago she'd faced this problem herself. The raft was proving too heavy to move. The girls planned to dig a trench to the pond, sluice the raft down the slippery slope, and push it into the water.

Henrietta glowed with pride! Those girls! So smart!

Not long after, pride turned to elation when she caught sight of the two poling away rapidly down the shore. Their work had been a success! The raft floated high and dry, just as it used to in her day.

Henrietta put down the binoculars and brought her palms together in silent applause. It was happening! It was all happening just as she'd wished and planned. Across the room Sally Parks had dozed off in her chair, unsuspecting. The newspaper she'd been reading had fallen off her lap onto the floor. Henrietta raised the binoculars again to keep watch.

She was rewarded a few hours later when she spotted the raft again. This time it was heading down the pond in the other direction, toward the beach. She lost sight of it when the girls turned into the reeds along the shore, across from the Coopers' stone chimney. A little while after, the pond girl came back alone, poling slowly, looking tired, as well she might after her efforts that morning. Henrietta stood up and waved. She wanted to be sure the pond girl would bring the raft back. She told her to come! *Come back to me!* she gestured.

But the mysterious line of communication between them seemed to have broken down. The girl passed far out into the middle of the pond without so much as a glance in Henrietta's direction.

Well, she'll soon return, Henrietta thought, to comfort herself. She sat back and closed her eyes. The day had worn her out as well.

The pond girl did not return that afternoon. Nor did she come the next morning, or the next afternoon. Or the morning after that. With every passing day Henrietta sank lower in her chair.

"I'm afraid I may have been forgotten," she told Sally, who patted her arm.

"Not at all. I'm always here."

Hour after hour she watched from the window, but the pond girl did not arrive. There was no sign of the other girl either. Both had disappeared. Minute by minute she expected their return, but they did not come.

"Miss Cutting, you've dropped your binoculars," Sally said. "And you're not looking yourself this afternoon. How about a little walk around the house? It would do you good to get up for a bit."

"No!"

And later, after supper, long after the sun had gone down: "Miss Cutting, you're not going to see anything out that window now. It's too dark."

"I hope I haven't been abandoned," Henrietta whispered, but in such a low voice that Sally Parks didn't hear.

Before Henrietta's eyes Sally bustled to and fro, folding down the yellow silk bedspread, puffing up the pillows, arranging the nightstand, drawing the blinds.

"There we are. Almost ready, dear?"

As it did every night, this meant bedtime, the moment when Henrietta usually put up a fight. Now she only nodded.

"I don't believe I'll need my sleep medicine tonight," she managed.

"Just as well," Sally replied. "That bottle's nearly done.

I'll be sure to call the pharmacy in the morning."

"I suppose I'll still be here in the morning. I am so tired," Henrietta murmured.

"Of course you will, Miss Cutting. What kind of talk is that?"

"I'd be grateful if you would please leave the night-light off this evening," Henrietta said. Or tried to say. The only word that came through clearly was "off," but Sally knew what she wanted.

The night-light was another bone of contention between them. Henrietta objected to the glow it threw around the room. She preferred the dark. Normally, Sally denied this request. The night-light made it easy to check on her charge from the hall. But tonight Miss Cutting looked so limp and unhappy, so unlike her usual prickly self, that Sally agreed. She would leave the light off, she said. Just for tonight.

"Safer," Henrietta murmured as Sally helped her into bed.

"Come again?"

"It's safer without the light," Henrietta mumbled.

She was tucked in. The light went off. Sally clumped out of the room, shut the door. Henrietta was left alone in the dark. She lay quiet, receptive, waiting for sleep to fold its wings around her. Her mother used to say that. As a child Henrietta had trouble falling asleep. There was so much energy left in her at the end of every day that she couldn't settle down. So much to think about, so much to do tomorrow.

"Lie back, darling. Let sleep fold you in its wings," her mother would whisper.

A kiss and she was gone. Too soon. Always a little too soon.

A loud bump out in the hall wakes her. Muffled voices. The sound of a struggle. Somebody shouts, "Walk! Get down those stairs!" Someone else makes a noise, a high noise. Her mother? Her father's voice booms out suddenly: "Who are you? What is this all about?"

There's another loud bump, then a grunt and a crash. Her mother's voice cries out: "Don't do that! Don't hit him!"

The struggling sounds continue, slowly descending the stairs. Henrietta is out of bed now. She runs to her bedroom door and peeks through the crack. At first the light in the hall is too bright and she can't see anything. Finally her eyes adjust and she sees a strange man's back heading down the stairs, away from her. He's wearing a cap over a full head of hair, and a gray overcoat. He shoves at something in front of him. Henrietta can't see what.

"I would like to know what this is all about," her father's voice says, strong and slow. "What is it you want? Money?"

"Nothing, pal," a rough voice says. "We already got ours."

Somebody laughs. A dry, coughing chuckle.

Henrietta runs to the hall banister and looks over. She crouches down behind it. Her father and mother are standing in their bedclothes in the downstairs foyer. The front door is wide open. The man in the cap and gray overcoat is looking over his shoulder at someone in the dining room. He says, "Not now. We'll get that stuff after."

"Hey, close that door," another voice says. "You want to wake up the whole world?"

Through the banister Henrietta can see only the feet of this speaker. Hunting boots laced up halfway. And wet. The leather is sodden. Gray with mud.

The person in the dining room comes into view, moving toward the front door. He closes it and turns around. He's wearing an overcoat too and has reddish hair, thinning on top. His trousers are stained and dirty. There's a gun in his hand, a large, dark pistol. He holds it out at arm's length in front of him.

Her father speaks, using the voice of reason Henrietta knows so well. He sounds so calm, so perfectly in control, that Henrietta relaxes her grip on the banister railing. Everything will be fine now. The problem will be fixed. In a moment she will run downstairs to her mother, or her mother will look up at her and smile. Her father speaks, steadily and clearly:

"There's no need for all this. Just tell us what you want. If someone has paid you, I will pay you more. Right now. I have cash upstairs. My wife has jewelry here. You can take what you like. There's plenty to go around. All three of you will find yourselves well compensated. The authorities need not know. We'll keep this among ourselves, shall we? Have we met before? I don't think we have. Let me introduce myself. I am George C. Cutting, president and owner of the *Providence Evening News*."

After his speech there's a long pause until the man with

the dry laugh laughs again. The man wearing the cap takes a step toward her father and says, "Sorry, buddy."

He has a bigger gun, one with a fat barrel. He raises it, tucks the back part against the gray overcoat, and fires with one hand, a tremendous blast. Henrietta jumps. The noise is like an earthquake. Her eyes squeeze shut. She tries to open them, but for some reason the lids are sealed against her face. She fights to open them before the next blast, the second one she knows is coming. If she could just open her eyes, she might stop this horrible dream. She might hold the universe still, go back in time to before any of this happened. . . .

The second explosion goes off and a whole world bursts inside her head. Henrietta screams, squashing her face between her hands. She screams and screams and screams and screams until a blinding light goes on suddenly.

A voice says: "Miss Cutting? Henrietta! Stop that! You are all right. I'm here, look at me. Look! It's me, Mrs. Parks. You've had another dream. It's just a dream. You're in bed. You've been asleep. There's nothing to be afraid of. That's better. Quiet now. Deep breaths. Calm yourself. You know these dreams. You know they're only dreams. There now, nothing can hurt you. It's only in your head. Only in your head. Only in your head. Only in your head."

In a little while, or perhaps it was a long while, Henrietta returned to the real world. She remembered that she was no longer the girl holding on to the banister in the hall. She remembered Sally Parks, who had gone down to the kitchen for a glass of juice and was now offering it to her as she lay stiffly, with knotted fists, on the bed. She sat up for a spoonful of sleep medicine and lay back on the pillows.

"I'm so sorry to bother you," she said to Sally in a low voice. And truly, she was sorry, ashamed that after all these years that dream, that terrible dream, should still find its way into her sleeping head.

"No bother," Sally said. "It's what I'm paid for. Don't worry yourself about it."

Henrietta nodded. "I think I'll sleep now."

"I'll leave the glass by your bed. In case you'd like another sip."

"Thank you."

"I think now we'd better have the night-light on," Sally said firmly.

Henrietta did not reply. She waited for Sally Parks to leave. When she was sure the woman had reached the far end of the hall (Sally slept in a room once reserved for her father's writer friends; Robert Frost had stayed there one time), Henrietta got up, crossed to the night-light, switched it off, and returned to bed. The dark was safer, she knew from experience. You could hide in the dark. Should someone come looking for you, they might not see you in a dark room, in a dark corner. If you were quiet, they might pass you by. You must not cry. You must barely breathe. You must freeze your body, freeze your mind. You must not move a muscle until the killers go away.

FOURTEEN

Sometime during the night the weather changed. Waking at five a.m. in his closet-size room, Richard Kettel heard the first rain of their summer vacation spattering against the screen. He got up to close the window and padded down the hall to the bathroom. He was coming back to bed when he heard a noise downstairs. A soft rustle of movement.

"Jessie?"

He thought it must be Jessie. She was the early riser in the house. Julia slept the sleep of the teenage dead until eight and beyond. Jonathan rarely woke before seven. He was growing so fast these days. It wasn't unusual for him to be out of commission for a solid ten hours.

"Jessica!"

There was no answer. The rustle had stopped.

Richard stood in his boxers at the top of the stairs and said his daughter's name a third time. When there was still no answer, he walked to his children's shared bedroom at the end of the hall and looked in.

They were both in bed, sound asleep. Julia was in her room too.

He returned to the stairs and walked boldly down. A draft of cool, damp air hit his face as he rounded into the dim living room. The long-necked lamps appeared almost human at first, wiry shapes standing guard over the couch. He looked past them into the kitchen and saw that the back door was wide open, swinging in the rainy breeze.

So that was it. The wind had worried the old wooden latch and blown the door open. He walked across the room and into the kitchen to close it.

A furtive movement in the pantry corner caught his eye. He spun around in time to see a small, lithe form stooped over the trash container, grubbing inside. The invader reared up, faced him with an animal snarl, and sprang for the door. Richard Kettel clutched the counter and cried out in alarm. By the time he'd recovered and raced to look outside, the thing was gone, slipped away into the dense vegetation that hid the pond.

A dog, he thought it was. A wild dog with small, pointed teeth and hungry eyes. "Ravenous" was the word he used to his children. Jessie arrived in the kitchen seconds later. A minute afterward Jonathan stumbled in. Both had been woken by their father's cry. Julia, of course, slept through the entire incident.

"All I know is the back door was closed when I came home," she said, a touch defensively, when she finally came down for breakfast around eight thirty.

"And what time was that, anyway?"

Her father, sipping his third espresso of the day at the kitchen table, gave her an accusing look. "What's happened to our midnight curfew?"

"Sorry. I know. I was a little late."

"A little! It was close to two a.m. by my clock."

"No, it wasn't, Dad! I was here long before one."

"Julia, I saw the headlights when you came back. It was definitely two a.m."

"What headlights? I wasn't in a car. I walked home from the beach."

Richard Kettel surveyed his daughter's face. "There were headlights that came down our driveway. What was it? A wrong turn?"

"Don't ask me. I was asleep." Julia's eyes landed hard on her father. "What, you don't believe me?"

"What can I say?"

"That you believe me."

"So, Dad, back to the main subject, what did come in our kitchen last night?" Jessie asked. "Was it really a dog?"

"Something was eating our garbage," her father said. "I don't know what. Maybe a big cat. It had a lot of gray hair."

"Philip said there's a family of foxes that lives across the pond," Jonathan said. "It could've been one of them. They make these horrible screaming sounds at night."

Julia nodded. "Actually, I might've heard that."

"When?"

"I don't know. A few nights ago. Late."

Her father spoke up. "Listen, Julia. I don't want you walking home by yourself from the beach anymore. Not at that hour. Get a ride with one of the kids, okay? It shouldn't be that hard."

"It isn't, except Aaron Bostwick keeps asking me and I don't want to ride with him. He doesn't talk. He just stares at me and waits for me to say something."

"So go with one of the girls. They've all got cars around here," her father said. "I've never seen so many kids with fancy cars and nothing to do. When I was young, we had bikes and summer jobs."

Jessie said, a little meanly, "How about Ripley Schute? I bet he has a Mercedes."

"Actually, he has a vintage Thunderbird." Julia swept her dark, sleep-tousled hair back from her face with both hands. "He isn't somebody you can just ask like that. He's kind of . . ."

"Older," Jessie said. "Oh yeah, that's right. He's going to Princeton in the fall."

"Shut up! It has nothing to do with that."

"A vintage Thunderbird. Wow! And Aaron Bostwick can't even talk."

"Well, he can't. Or he doesn't. You were there, you saw him. Nobody in our group can stand him. He's a weirdo."

"Another weirdo. There are so many around here."

"I am not the only one who thinks that!"

It was as this conversation was heating up in the kitchen that their father, entering the living room, made another discovery. His laptop was not in its usual place.

"It was on the coffee table last night," he said from the

living room. "Did somebody borrow it?" He came back and gazed at his three children, who all shook their heads.

Jessie said, "Are you sure you didn't take it upstairs?"

He definitely had not. A trip to his room proved him right. The laptop was not in the kitchen, not in the bathroom, not fallen down behind a chair. It was not anywhere in the house.

Jonathan said eagerly, "I bet somebody stoled it. In the night!"

A ridiculous statement.

Until they began to think about it. The lights at two a.m. The back door wide open.

"Hey, Dad. Could the animal that was eating our garbage have stolen your laptop?"

"Julia, please! This is serious."

"The animal must've come in after," Jessie said. "It probably smelled the garbage and came in. The back door must've already been open. Some person must've come in."

"Someone came in our house last night?" Julia looked alarmed.

"What about the headlights you saw?" Jessie asked her father.

"Well, I thought it was headlights because I thought it was Julia coming home. I was half-asleep."

"It could've been a flashlight," Julia said. "That would make more sense. Especially if someone was sneaking around here in the dark." She sent Jessie a meaningful glance. "If that someone found the back door unlocked, which it always is, they just might have decided to come in—"

"Wait a minute," Jessie interrupted.

"And look around. And there's this nice laptop just sitting on—"

"What are you saying, Julia?"

"Well, there's only one person I know of who hangs around this house at strange hours watching us."

"She has never been in this house," Jessie said. "She wouldn't do that."

"Oh really?" Julia's dark lashes curved into crescents. "Did you know she got caught at a CVS shoplifting some stuff?"

"That was a mistake. She forgot to pay."

"Oh, right. She walked out with a load of stuff in a back-pack and she forgot to pay?"

"How do you know that?"

"People in town know about her, about her family. They know at the beach, too."

"Well, what did she take?"

"Everything, I guess. Books, pens, lipstick, skin cream. What would you take from a CVS?"

"I don't know, Julia. What would you take?"

"I wouldn't bother taking anything," Julia sniffed. "There's nothing in a CVS that's worth the risk of doing that. Except drugs, which I guess she didn't take. If she'd stolen them, she wouldn't be hanging around here at all. She'd already be in jail."

"Okay, okay, that's enough." Their father stepped between

them. "I'm sure Terri did not steal my laptop. Why would she? Jessie is her friend."

"I don't know," Julia said, "but I bet I'm right. And anyway, where is she this morning?"

Jonathan ran across the living room to the front door and tugged it open. "Not here!" he yelled back.

Julia nodded. "So there you are."

FIFTEEN

Jessie knew the safest thing would be to stay away from Terri Carr.

She didn't think Terri was a bad person. She didn't believe she'd stolen the laptop. It was everything else that made up the frightening swamp around her: her violent father; her desperate family; their hopeless, dead-end lives. No wonder Terri thought she had to carry a knife. And shoplifting. Of course anyone who had to steal from her own father might turn to that. Jessie didn't blame Terri. She sympathized with her and felt sorry that she was stuck where she was. She just didn't want to get any closer.

For a while it seemed possible that she wouldn't have to. The raft was in Terri's hands now, which made it fair to call it quits. Terri had taken the raft back up the pond to her house. Or she was somewhere hiding out on it, living on it the way she'd said she wanted to. When three days went by without any sign of her, Jessie began to believe that she'd disappeared for good, and she was relieved. The break-in at the garage had rattled her. The more she thought about it, the more she saw how close she'd come to real danger. She might have run into some druggies up there and been hurt. She might be dragged in even now, accused of stealing if the police found the track leading down to the pond.

"Still no Terri," Jonathan would say, looking out the front door in the mornings. He'd say it to Jessie in the kitchen at breakfast, and again to Julia when she appeared an hour later.

"Right," Julia answered one morning. "It's more and more obvious that she did it. Dad should report her to the police. She was never your friend, Jessie. She wanted our stuff. She got our laptop and now she's taken off."

"Jessie, could that be true?" her father said. He liked Terri. He didn't want to involve her if he didn't have to.

"No! It's not true!"

Jessie wanted to end things with Terri, but she didn't want to lie about her. She explained again: "Look, the reason Terri's not here is because of something that happened between us. We decided to go our separate ways. It has nothing to do with the laptop."

Julia laughed. "You're trying to protect her."

"I'm not!"

"Well, everyone I've told says there's absolutely no doubt she's the one. She has a reputation."

"Why are you telling people anything? It's none of their business!"

"It's everybody's business when somebody starts breaking into houses."

"Julia! That is so arrogant. You can't talk that way about a person when you're not even sure."

"But I am sure, Jessie. There's nobody else. Terri has stolen stuff before and she'll do it again. Dad, you should call the police. You should call them right now!"

"All right, all right." He gave in at last. He wouldn't telephone. Everything sounded so drastic on the phone. "I'll go up to the station and have a friendly chat. Anyone want to come with me?"

"Me! Me!" Jonathan said. "I've never been in a police station."

"You can go if you behave and keep quiet," his father said. "Jessie, why don't you come too? I'd think that you'd want to get out of the house for a change."

"No, thank you," Jessie said. The thought of the police made her sick.

"She won't go," Julia said. "She's planning to spend the rest of this vacation moping in her room. She's already been in there for three solid days."

"Shut up, Julia. Why don't you go with Dad? You're the one who's accusing everybody."

"I would, but I promised Rip I'd meet him at the beach. He's taking me to play tennis at the club later."

"Coward!" Jessie said, and stormed upstairs.

She wasn't moping in her room, she was reading. No she wasn't, she was writing a letter to her mother. Except the letter wouldn't start. Too much had happened. Then, unexpectedly, she was writing to Terri. She was explaining why things hadn't worked out between them, even though she really liked Terri and had wanted things to work.

The trouble was (Jessie wrote) that she was way behind on her summer reading and had to stay home to do it.

The trouble was that their friendship had no future, since Jessie lived in Pittsburgh and would probably never be back to this town again.

The trouble was that they came from different kinds of families, families that wouldn't get along, that were on completely different wavelengths and understood different things about how the world worked and . . .

Jessie tore up the letter and threw it away.

The trouble was, she couldn't get Terri Carr out of her mind.

She sat on her bed with a book in her lap and worried about her. She kept an eye out the window in case the raft came past. Once, she thought she saw a figure on the pond in the distance. She ran for the binoculars, which were all the way downstairs. By the time she got back, the figure was gone, if it had ever been there, for a strange thing had begun to happen.

The more invisible Terri was, the more Jessie began to see her anyway. She saw her in her dark, run-down house at the end of the pond, and in the CVS with a backpack. She saw her in the school bathroom when everyone ran out. She saw her when the barn burned and her brothers were accused, and people looked at her and thought her family had done it.

She saw Terri in all these situations, and then she began

to hear her. Terri was out there somewhere on the pond. She was waiting for Jessie to send her a sign, to tell her it was okay, they could start over.

"I thought you were on my side," Jessie heard Terri say. "I thought we were fixing up the raft for both of us. We had this great thing going. After everything we did, don't you care anymore?"

The trouble was, Jessie cared.

Richard Kettel was not enthusiastic about going to the police. If Julia hadn't made such a fuss, he might not have bothered. All this finger-pointing over an inexpensive laptop (it was a cheap model) that he wasn't using anyway because he was now writing by hand and the computer couldn't access the Internet.

"Are you going to tell them who did it?" Jonathan asked on the drive up. "Are you going to say it was Terri?"

"No, because we don't know it was. And you are not to say a word while we're in there, is that clear? You are just a listener."

"Okay," Jonathan agreed. "But can I look at the jail after-wards? I never saw one in real life."

"I don't think there is one there," his father said. "When they make an arrest, they take the perpetrator up to Providence or somewhere."

"What's a perpetrator?" Jonathan asked, yanking on his seat belt. It hit him too high and pinched the skin on his neck.

"It's the guy that's charged with committing the crime."

"Or the girl, if Terri did it, right?"

"Enough about Terri. We're not going to talk about her, remember?"

The station was in a century-old building at the center of town that also housed the fire department. After Jonathan had inspected the two old-fashioned hook and ladders, they went over to the law enforcement side. A police officer in shirtsleeves took down Richard Kettel's information.

"So you believe this was a break-in?"

"Well, they didn't actually break in. They came in. The back door was more or less open."

"So this door has no lock?"

"Well, yes. There is a lock, but we didn't think we needed it. The house—it's a cottage, really—is way down a dirt road near Quicksand Pond."

"The old Lopes place?"

"I don't know what it's called. It's right on the pond. Kind of in disrepair. We've been renting it."

"That's the Lopes place. You have any idea who might have come in and taken your computer, sir?"

"Well, no. We don't." Richard Kettel placed a firm hand on Jonathan's neck. "We don't know, but we thought it was a good idea to report it. Have there been any other break-ins around there recently?"

"Nothing that's come to our attention so far. That cottage is real out of the way. I wouldn't think it'd attract thieves.

Have you got other items in the house that could raise fast money?"

"Raise what?"

"That could be turned over quick, fenced. If someone did take your laptop, sir, it would probably be for the resale. People around here aren't into computers. Internet connection isn't too hot."

"I know."

Richard began to feel the futility of the whole visit.

"I can send a man down to investigate."

"No, no. That will not be necessary. This happened a few days ago."

"Then I suggest you contact your rental agency about improving security at the house. In the meantime, we'll keep an eye out for your lost item, though I'd say there's not much chance of recovering it now. If there's another incident, it'd be helpful if you called in sooner."

"Yes, thank you. We'll do that."

With the main business attended to, Jonathan would no longer be contained. His small body erupted from the chair and his voice rang out.

"Do you have a jail in here?"

The officer smiled. It was the kind of question people of all ages asked. "We do. A single cell for overnight emergencies. It's in the back."

"Can I see it?"

"It's occupied today. So no, not today. Maybe another time."

"What emergency did they do?"

"What?"

"What did they do that got them put in?"

"Sorry, sonny. That's information I can't give out."

The officer smiled apologetically, but Jonathan pressed on.

"Well, is it a girl? If it's a girl, maybe she's already been—"

"Jonathan!" Richard Kettel collared his son and marched him out to the car.

At home he checked the locks. The kitchen door had an old-fashioned slide bolt that seemed perfectly adequate against intruders, both two-legged and four. (The horrifying image of that hairy creature, whatever it was, rooting in the trash with its needle-sharp teeth kept preying on his mind.)

The front door had a weathered dead bolt for which there was only one key. He'd give it to Julia when she went out that evening with instructions to lock back up when she came home. She'd probably lose it on the beach, of course, and end up pounding on the door at midnight to get in.

I'll get another from the rental agency and have it duplicated, Richard promised himself, though it seemed ridiculous to be locking the front door of a house so far off the beaten track. The loss of one second-rate laptop, probably now in the hands of the vanished Terri Carr, seemed hardly worth worrying about.

The truth was, he felt sorry for Terri. Maybe she hadn't stolen the laptop to sell. Maybe she wanted it for herself, for schoolwork this coming fall. She looked like a bright kid. Perhaps a computer was the one thing that would change her life, improve her grades, make it possible for her to get into a good college on scholarship. You hoped for escapes like that with those kinds of people, those hard-luck cases.

That evening Richard Kettel slipped the slide bolt into place on the back door, left the front door open in case Julia lost the key, and went upstairs to bed in a generous frame of mind.

SIXTEEN

The Kettels' vacation entered the month of August with more rain and such fierce humidity that the pond sprouted an evil-looking greenish scum.

Jessie's mother called on Saturday morning and reported that the city was blazing hot. She sounded drained on the phone. After a hushed conversation behind the kitchen door, their father returned to say, "Your mother looked us up on a map. She saw the pond. She saw our house. I think she misses us!"

"Is she coming?" Jonathan asked. "I want her to come."

"I asked her to. I told her she'd have two weeks if she came now. She said she'd think about it. We'll have to be patient and wait and see."

"But where would she sleep?" Jonathan wanted to know. "There're no more beds."

"I guess we'd have to figure that out when the time came," his father answered in a voice that told Jessie he didn't expect he'd have to.

"I'm driving to town today," he went on more brightly.

"I'm dropping Jonathan at Philip's house and then heading to the town library to do some background work. Anybody want to come? There's Internet up there."

"There is? You never said!" Julia ran to brush her hair and put on her sandals.

"Jessie? We could have lunch there in the little diner. They have lobster rolls."

"No thanks. I'll stay here."

"Sure?"

She was.

A short while later her family had climbed into the car and driven off. The house turned silent. She went back to her room and gazed out the window.

An hour went by. Then a second hour. As a third began, Jessie found she could not for a moment longer be patient and wait and see about Terri Carr. She had to find her right away. There was something she needed to say. She set off on foot around the edge of the pond. She hadn't gone far when she came across a sort of camp near the bank.

Someone had made a fire. A few pieces of blackened wood were lying on the ground, still smoking. A plastic lawn chair was set up nearby. A flat rock had been laid over two other rocks to make a low table. Jessie sat down in the lawn chair. Not long after, she heard the scrape of the raft coming through the reeds.

Terri showed no surprise at finding her there. She brought the raft neatly into the bank and jumped off in a business-like way, without a greeting. Her clothes were sodden and dirty. Her black hair hung in tangles around her face. She set down a brown paper bag on the stone table.

"I got bug spray," she said without looking up. "You know, it's not so bad outside at night as you'd think. After dark the worst is over."

"Are you sleeping here now?" Jessie asked politely.

"Been here three nights," Terri said. "Mitch has been on a tear. I've been keeping my head down."

"So you can't go home?"

"I've been home. Just not when he's there." She glanced at Jessie. "Hey, it's not his fault, okay? I riled him. I forget sometimes how to handle him. I should know by now. I've lived with him my whole life."

Jessie could think of no way to answer this. She let a minute go by and started again.

"Well, how's the raft holding up?"

"Look for yourself. It's floating high and dry. I got all the way to the old Indian dam. Saw a big snapper."

"A what?"

"A snapping turtle. You don't see them too much these days. They're shy, but you have to watch out. You wouldn't want to go swimming with one of those around. It could snap onto your arm or your leg and drag you down. Once a snapper has ahold of you, there's no getting him off unless you shoot him. And even then he won't let go for a few hours."

"A few hours! Even if he's dead?"

"You know what? A snapper's body can walk around without a head. And the head can snap without a body. I saw it happen to a dog one time. He got bit by getting too close to the severed head."

"I don't believe it."

"Well, it happened. I saw it!"

The air between them warmed. Terri relaxed and grinned, revealing the whole expanse of her crooked brown teeth. Jessie smiled too, but warily.

"Are you really sleeping out here? Aren't you afraid?"

"Of what?"

"I don't know, snakes?"

"There aren't any poisonous ones around here."

"Quicksand?"

"Give me a break."

"No sign of the Peckham boys, I guess."

"Nope."

They looked at each other and laughed.

"Listen, it's beautiful here," Terri said. "Yesterday around sunset there were these huge flocks of starlings that swooped around over the pond. They make amazing patterns high up in the sky, hundreds of birds all turning at once, like a cloud ballet. Have you ever seen that? Then night came and the stars got so bright. I just lay back and let it happen, like a movie. You should try it."

"Sounds amazing."

"You should do it soon, before you have to go home. I bet where you live has nothing like this."

"I'd have to persuade my dad. He won't even let Julia walk home from the beach at night."

"So don't tell him," Terri said. "Sneak out after he's asleep. I do that all the time. I'll bring an extra blanket for you to lie on."

"Maybe," Jessie said. "I'll think about it."

Terri began taking supplies out of the paper bag: chips, apples, juice boxes, sandwich bread, hot dogs. She held up a Milky Way bar.

"Want to split it? I got another one too. You could have a whole one if you want."

"No thanks. But thanks."

"You are one hard nut," Terri said, shaking her head. "I never can give you anything you want to share."

She sat down on the ground, unwrapped the candy bar, and began to eat it. Jessie went over and sat beside her. They both looked at the pond.

"How long are you going to stay out here?" Jessie asked.

"I don't know. Until I feel like going back. I've even been cooking here! Well, hot dogs mostly."

"I saw your fire. That's how I knew somebody was here."

"I use starter fluid to get it going. And now I don't even need matches, because I've got this."

From under the stone table Terri brought out a wand-like utensil that turned out to be a fire lighter.

"Pretty cool, right? You can light anything with this." She flicked a switch and a fiery tongue leaped out. "It's the only thing that really works in the wind. I picked it up a couple of days ago at the hardware store."

She caught a look on Jessie's face and added, "Not like that.

I had money. I paid for it, if that's what you're wondering."

"I wasn't."

"Yes, you were."

"No, really." Jessie took a breath. "There's something else. Something you should know that happened at our house. We got robbed. Someone came in at night and stole a laptop from our living room. My dad went and reported it to the police."

Terri said nothing. She pressed her lips together and turned her face toward the pond.

"I know you didn't do it," Jessie said quickly, "but my family thinks that's the reason you haven't been around. You were always there before, and now, well, it looks bad."

"How do you know I didn't do it?" Terri said, staring at the pond.

"I told them why you weren't coming anymore, that it was because of a different reason. I said the reason was just between us."

"Just between us."

"Well, it was really me. I'm sorry I said that about your plumbing and your family. I don't know why I did except I got nervous. About the tools and the garage, and that someone might think it was us."

Terri was silent. One hand had risen up to her name charm.

"Anyway, I thought you should know what happened at our house in case somebody says something. So you aren't surprised or anything."

"Surprised?" Terri scoffed. "Who's surprised? At school when anything's missing, guess who they call into the office? I bet you can't guess."

Jessie herself did a surprising thing then, something she didn't expect to do. She reached out and touched Terri's hand, the one that was holding the name charm. She covered Terri's hand with hers.

"I know you didn't do it," she whispered.

Terri nodded. She got up and walked away to the raft and began to kick it methodically with one foot. The heavy platform rocked and bobbed in the water, sending out ripples into the reeds, which rattled against other reeds and shook their tufted heads.

"You don't have to worry about the tools anymore," she said over her shoulder. "I went up there and took care of it."

"You put them back?"

"Yes."

"In the garage?"

"Yes."

"That's so great! I never would've dared."

Terri shrugged. "I went after dark."

"How did it look in there? Had they taken more stuff?"

"I couldn't see. It was pitch black. I just threw in the tools and left."

"You must've had to make a few trips. There were a lot!"

"I did."

Jessie gazed at her in full admiration. When it came right down to it, Terri carried through. She didn't make a big deal of it. She just went ahead and figured out how to do what needed to be done. Like fixing the raft, or handling her father. Or camping out by herself when she couldn't go home.

"Thanks so much, Terri. That's a big relief."

"That's why I did it. I knew the tools were worrying you."

"They were. Thank you."

Terri smiled. "So, we're friends again, right? I'm so glad you came. I was hoping you would because I have this great trip all planned out for us."

"A trip?"

"There's this old pet cemetery behind a house up the road. You've got to see it! It has dogs and cats and a rabbit that was named Jumper, and even somebody's goldfish. They're all buried with little crosses and RIP signs inside an iron fence with a green gate. We could take the raft up the pond and sneak into it."

"Is it on somebody's land?"

"It's behind a house, but they'd never see us. It's like a jungle around there."

Jessie looked at her.

"Really! I go there all the time. I buried Mungo there."

"Who's Mungo?"

"Our cat that died of rat poison. I took him over last year and dug his grave and nobody even knows. He was a great cat. I wanted him to be with all those other pets. We can visit him!"

"He ate rat poison?"

"Somebody gave it to him is what I think. Someone lured him with food and tricked him."

"They poisoned your cat? That's sick!"

"I know."

"That person must really hate you to do that. Can't you report them?"

Terri shrugged. "You can't get people arrested for killing a cat. The best I could do was take Mungo to a good place to get buried. He doesn't have a marker, but he's in that ground. He's got honor."

"Honor?"

"Like the other pets. He had a real big heart. He trusted people too much, that's what got him into trouble. Worse than that, it got him killed."

Jessie came to a sudden decision.

"I can't go today," she said. "I've got to get home today."

"Okay, but sometime, right?"

"Sometime."

"How about just a short trip now? I was going to pole over to see the baby foxes. I have some crusts!" Terri held up a plastic bag. "You don't have to leave yet, do you? You just got here."

"Thanks, but . . ."

"Because we're safe now," Terri insisted. "I made us safe. No one's ever going to know about the tools."

"I know. It's not that. Just, another time would be better. I'll let you know."

"How?"

"I'll just come here."

"I don't know how much longer I'm going to be at this camp," Terri said.

"I'll call you. On my cell phone."

"You have a cell phone?"

"Yes."

"Well, give me your number. I can call you! We can stay in touch. I don't want to show up at your house anymore anyway if everyone thinks I stole your laptop."

"Oh, Terri, I'm sorry."

"It's okay. Just give me your number and I'll call you every couple of days. You can say whether it's a good time to go out on the raft or not. If it's not, don't worry. I can wait."

"Terri . . ."

"So tell me your number. I can remember without writing it down. I have a mind like a steel trap. Mitch says that."

"Terri . . ." Jessie looked away. A strange silence opened between them.

Terri said, "Oh, I get it. You don't want to."

"Anyway, my cell doesn't work at our house. I just remembered," Jessie said, not meeting her eyes.

For a moment Terri looked crushed. Her lips parted and her forehead buckled, as if she might be on the verge of pleading, or even bursting into tears. In the end she folded her arms across her chest, lifted her chin, and spoke in a high, proud voice.

"You know, I'm not going to be stuck here forever. I'm going to get out of this someday."

"Sure," Jessie said. "I know you will."

"No, you don't understand. I'm going to be awesome. You'll want to be friends when you see how great I'll be. I'll do stuff you won't believe. I'm getting better and I'm getting out."

"I know. I know you will."

"You don't believe me."

"Yes, I do! I just have to go right now."

Jessie turned to walk away, and Terri, standing with her arms still folded across her chest, let her go. She allowed her to get a good distance down the shore, almost out of sight, before calling to her.

"Hey, Jessie. You know, your dad is right about not letting Julia walk home at night. And he might not want to let her drive home with anyone either."

Jessie turned around. "What do you mean?"

"Some of those beachers are really bad news. Julia probably can't tell the difference between the good guys and the creeps."

"She thinks she can tell."

"Well, you know who she's hanging out with now, don't you?"

"Who?" Jessie walked back a little way to hear better.

"Ripley Schute. He comes here every summer and picks on some girl who doesn't know anything, who's impressed by his car and his superrich dad."

"So, what does his dad do?"

"Owns a bank probably, I don't know. He's in some business in Providence. That family has been around here for years, pulling all kinds of stunts. They used to work a dairy like us, but they sold out. They'd never admit they did anything like farming, though. They've risen up too high. You should tell Julia to steer clear of Rip. She's kind of an inno-cent person, anybody can see. He's a real low-level creep. He got a girl in trouble last summer."

"He did?"

"His dad paid to have it taken care of, you know what I mean?"

Jessie knew. "I'll tell Julia," she said. "Thanks for letting us know. Actually, I think she's a little afraid of him."

"I would be if I were her," Terri said. "I'd be scared stiff. He's like that snapper up at the dam, just waiting for some-one to fall in the water."

SEVENTEEN

Julia and Richard Kettel had arrived at the village center and were just getting out of their car to go into the library when Julia pointed.

"Look! Look who I see."

Her father took a moment to recognize the disheveled figure coming through the door of the village market.

"It's Terri Carr," Julia breathed. "She looks like she's been in a swamp."

She did. Her hair was slicked back behind her ears, wet and scraggly. Her shirt and jean shorts were filthy. She wore rubber flip-flops too big for her feet. They slapped loudly against her soles as she walked. She was carrying groceries in a brown paper bag.

Julia turned her back. "Don't let her see us. We don't want to talk to her."

But Richard could tell that Terri wasn't about to talk to anyone. Just the opposite: her eyes were on the ground and she was walking away as fast as she could. She crossed the street and cut in behind the old white-steepled church. The last he saw of her, she was heading downhill toward the elementary school. Going home, he supposed.

"Poor kid," he said. "She leads a rough life."

Julia snorted. "You are such a bleeding heart. She probably stole our laptop, you know."

Her father shook his head. "Even if she did, I feel sorry for her."

"Well, I don't. I'm just glad Jessie isn't hanging out with her anymore. She is not someone we want to fool around with."

Richard Kettel was visited by a sudden realization. "You know, I think I might have known her father when I was here as a kid."

He'd been vaguely aware of this possibility for some time but kept pushing the notion aside. Now it rose with more certainty.

"She even looks a little like how I remember him back then."

"Who?" Julia demanded.

"Mitch. Mitch . . . Carr. Of course! That was his name! Mitchell Carr. Well, that's certainly a coincidence. I wonder what he's doing now?"

"Dad! You don't want to know, okay? That's Terri's family down at the end of the pond. They're not good people."

Her father's curiosity had been aroused, however. In the library that morning, while Julia settled down in front of an impossibly slow and backward computer (though at least it had Internet), he casually interviewed the librarian on duty.

Did she happen to know the Carr family? The one that lived down on Quicksand Pond?

She did. Everybody in town knew them. Because of the trouble the boys were always in, and the girl wasn't much better. And then their old barn burning down under suspicious circumstances. Though no one was ever charged. But people in a town like this knew things whether or not the law caught up. There was court judgment that had to be proved beyond a doubt, and then there was what people knew. The Carr family, Richard learned, was in the second category of what people knew.

"That family's had trouble from way back," the librarian said. "There was a big murder in this town years ago. It was all over the newspapers from here to Boston. The Carrs were involved in that, too. You can look it up if you want. We've got a whole file of stuff here in the library."

The next thing Richard knew, he wasn't working on background for his novel anymore. He was in the library archives, which occupied a basement room beneath the main building. He was poring over folders full of clippings and reading old newspapers on an ancient microfilm reader that dated from, what, fifty years ago?

"I didn't know these machines still existed," he told the helpful librarian.

"You wouldn't believe the stuff that's still around in this town," she answered. "People here don't let go easily. They like to hang on to things. You can't tell them there's a better way of thinking. They don't want to hear it."

*　　*　　*

Home from the library that afternoon, Richard Kettel waited until Julia had left for the beach before speaking to Jessie about what he'd found. Anything to do with the Carrs sent his elder daughter into a righteous rage. He waited until after lunch, when Jonathan, back from a strenuous morning of swimming with Philip, was temporarily at low ebb in the living room.

"I did a little poking around on your murder this morning," he said quietly to Jessie in the kitchen.

"My murder! Why is it mine?"

"You asked me about it, didn't you? Well, I found some interesting information in the library. From old newspaper clippings. You know that huge house down the pond? It was owned by one of the richest men in the state, a newspaper magnate named George C. Cutting. In 1944 there was a robbery there. He and his wife were shot dead. A dairyman named Eddie Carr was arrested and went to prison. He was Terri's great-grandfather."

"I already know that," Jessie said. "Terri told me. She said he didn't do it."

"Well, he looks pretty guilty from these clippings. Remember the friend I worked with on trash that summer? The kid who took me fishing? I figured out he was Mitch Carr. Remember how I said the family drove to Pennsylvania one time to visit someone in prison? They must've been visiting Eddie Carr. He was still alive then, I guess."

Jessie gazed at her father. "Dad! You're so hopeless. I already know all this."

"You knew Terri's father was the guy I went fishing with? Why didn't you tell me?"

Jessie sighed. "I didn't tell Terri, either. I didn't think you and Mitch would get along, the way things are with him. He's a big drunk now and their place is a mess. I was afraid you might try to go over there or something."

Her father looked away thoughtfully. "I should've figured out who she was. There was something familiar about Terri right from the beginning. I guess I just didn't want to think about it. It's one of those sad situations you don't want to dwell on."

Jessie measured her father with a glance and decided to take the conversation one step further.

"I've been feeling bad about Terri too," she said. "I went to see her today. She's camped out by herself on the pond. She can't go home until Mitch cools down. They had some kind of fight. He gets drunk and . . ."

"Poor kid," Richard said for the second time that day. "I wish we could do something."

"I do too," Jessie said. "The trouble is it's really complicated with her. You can't just be her friend in a normal way. The more you know her, the more you get kind of sucked into her life."

Her father's head swung around. "But you haven't . . ." He stopped and rephrased. "I mean, everything's okay, isn't it? You've been out with her on that raft a few times and that's it, right?"

"Oh, sure," Jessie said quickly. "Everything's fine. I

can see how it might turn into a problem though."

Her father nodded. "You know what? I think the best thing would be for you to keep some distance between you and Terri. From now on, I mean. Your mother would say that. She'd be worried you might be drawn into an uncomfortable situation. It might sound callous, but you have to be careful in cases like this. You have to protect yourself."

"It's hard, because I really like Terri," Jessie said. "I like her very much."

"I know," her father said. "We all do. It's one of those sad things."

A shout came from the living room. Jonathan was gearing up again. He'd dragged out the Monopoly game they'd brought from Pittsburgh and was demanding to play. Immediately!

"I printed out some of the articles about the murders, if you're interested," her father went on quickly. "I guess the daughter was asleep upstairs when it happened. There's a photo of her."

"There is?"

"She had a breakdown of some kind afterwards. Did you know she still lives in town?"

"She lives here on the pond," Jessie said. "In that same big house. I've met her, actually. She's a little crazy but not completely out of it. She came down to see us when we were . . ."

She put her hand over her mouth.

Better not to tell that secret. Better not to say a word, even with the tools returned. Her father seemed not to have heard, anyway. Jonathan was raising a din in the living room, calling for them to get started on the game, that he wanted to be the banker. Jessie's father thrust the articles into her hand and went to quell the storm.

"Okay, okay! If you're going to be the banker, you need to give me two thousand dollars to start off with. No, those are the hundred-dollar bills. The orange ones are the five-hundred-dollar bills. Give me three five hundreds and three one-hundred-dollar bills and then—"

"Don't you want to play?" Jonathan yelled as Jessie disappeared upstairs.

No, she said. Not this time. No.

The girl in the newspaper photo was unrecognizable. She looked nothing like the ghostly figure who'd surprised them at the pond. Old age had erased every feature from Henrietta Cutting's appearance back then: her light, curly hair; her oval face; her pale eyes and determined chin. Jessie wondered if this could really be the same person, this long-legged girl caught at the foot of some porch steps, a fishing pole cocked over a shoulder.

The photo must have been taken before the murders, Jessie thought. The girl was gazing straight at the camera, an impatient look on her face, as if she was being interrupted. She'd stand still for this moment, her expression said, but no longer. She had better things to do and places to be. Another minute and she'd be on her way.

The newspaper headline presented another reality:

CUTTING DAUGHTER TRAPPED IN HOUSE WHILE KILLERS ROAMED.

She'd suffered some collapse during police questioning and was never called to testify at the trial, according to the news story. As the thieves ransacked the house, she'd hidden. A housekeeper arriving the next morning came upon her parents' bodies in the front hall. The girl was found later, huddled under a dressing table upstairs.

"She didn't know me," the housekeeper was quoted as saying. "When we came upon her, she didn't move. She couldn't speak. Frozen, she was, like a block of ice."

Other photos showed Mr. and Mrs. Cutting as they had looked in life, a well-padded middle-aged couple attending various Providence social events. There was a photo of Mr. Cutting in a business suit visiting his newspaper offices, surrounded by his writers and reporters. Eddie Carr was not pictured, except for one long-range shot showing a short, stocky figure—it must have been him—being brought into court between a pair of police officers.

LOCAL DAIRYMAN CONVICTED IN CUTTING MURDERS, one headline read.

Jessie wondered if Terri had seen these articles. She thought not. They so directly contradicted her version of events. According to the articles, Eddie Carr was caught practically red-handed with the stolen property. A neighboring farmer had tipped off the police. He'd been up late with an ailing cow, he testified, and seen suspicious activity at the Carrs' landing.

Everything was there under a tarp on Eddie's dock. His boat showed evidence of bloody boot prints. A cap of the sort he was known to wear was found nearby, spattered with blood. More incriminating, a jewelry box belonging to Mrs. Cutting was recovered in a woodbin on the Carrs' back porch.

"We got our man," the chief of police was quoted as saying. "It's an open-and-shut case. The guy never had time to get rid of the goods."

Testifying for himself, Eddie protested it all. He knew nothing of the jewelry box, he said. The cap wasn't his. His boat had been tampered with. He'd been asleep all night in his own bed—just ask his wife!

The prosecuting attorney called him a liar. His wife wept on the stand and could barely be heard. The murder weapon was never found. ("Likely sunk in the pond," the prosecutor surmised.) The jury convicted and recommended death, but when the sentence was read, the judge spared Eddie's life.

Eddie Carr had had a clean record up till then, was the reason given. He came from a landholding family. It was living next to all that wealth that had deviled his mind. The Cuttings' summer estate had more in common with the mansions of Newport than with the working farms surrounding it. A man might be angered by such extravagance. A man might be tempted, during hard times, to steal for the good of his family. But murder? For murder there was no justification. For that Eddie would spend the rest of his natural life incarcerated in a federal prison.

Jessie stopped reading. She went back to Henrietta's photo. There, after a second examination, she saw that what she'd thought was a fishing pole had no reel or line. It was just a long, smooth shaft big enough to fit neatly into the girl's palm.

Jessie glanced at Henrietta's shoes. They were old-fashioned lace-up canvas sneakers, dark and soggy-looking. Above them Henrietta's bare legs extended to a pair of floppy, old-fashioned shorts. More telling, her legs showed streaks of mud, the same mud Jessie often found on her own legs when she came in from a day on the water.

"She's been on a raft," Jessie said out loud. "She's been out poling around on the pond!"

Her first thought was to find Terri and show her: *Look at this! Henrietta Cutting isn't as crazy as we thought. She really did have a raft. She thought ours was hers, that's why she came down to see us. That's why she's been trying to help us fix it up. She wants us to do something for her. But what? We should visit her and find out.*

In the end, though, Jessie didn't go. She agonized for an hour, then thought better of it. To go was to take another step toward the Carrs' messy life at the end of the pond. To go was to start up again with Terri, who'd expect her to do things that might get her in trouble. Jessie decided to play it safe and stay home. That evening she was glad she had, because another crisis was already under way at the beleaguered Cutting mansion.

EIGHTEEN

Henrietta was in her bedroom upstairs when she smelled smoke. A mild whiff sifting through the screen, as if someone was doing a bit of local burning. She paid no attention, for just at that moment the raft came into view! She nearly fell out of her chair trying to get the binoculars focused.

So much time had passed since she'd seen the raft that at first she wondered if she was imagining things. There were moments when the world she saw with her own eyes and the worlds that appeared before the eyes inside her head overlapped. They came together and fused with frightening ease. No world seemed entirely safe from intrusion by another. None was absolutely reliable.

But there was the raft! She saw it clearly, proceeding in all its glory across the middle of the pond. Henrietta was overjoyed. Only the dark-haired pond girl was aboard. She was poling hard, seemingly headed for the overgrown bog on the other side.

Henrietta recalled that secluded place in bright detail.

Great blue herons used to live there. Also, an immense number of frogs. And once, a pair of gray foxes came out on the bank, lowered their sleek heads, and lapped at the edge. She'd watched, holding her breath from behind a curtain of reeds.

The best thing about a raft was how quiet it was, how you could slip around a bend and catch wild things unaware. As she watched the pond girl pole across the water, Henrietta was filled with a longing so pure and painful that she gasped for air. She wished more than anything to be out there again, to see and feel the pond beneath her feet.

I must waste no more time. I must take possession of my raft again, make contact with the girls, plan my escape. Wait any longer and they'll forget all about me!

A strong smell of burning stung her nostrils. She lowered the binoculars in time to see smoke drifting around the side of the house. Great billows of it.

"Mrs. Parks! Oh, Mrs. Parks!"

The woman was a perfect loss to humanity. Never around when she should be. Always off in some distant corner of the house.

Henrietta rose laboriously from her chair and went out to the hall. She called again and was attempting to descend the stairs by herself when Mrs. Parks's ponderous form shot into view.

"Stay where you are, Miss Cutting! We have an emergency on our hands!"

"I smell smoke," Henrietta called out. "Something's on fire."

"I've phoned the fire department! Stay upstairs!" Sally shouted back.

Well, that was a ridiculous order. Henrietta was not the sort of person who stayed upstairs while something in her house was on fire. She came down slowly, step by step, recalling for some reason the bonfires her father used to set. He was a great clearer of property. Liked to be out in his leather work boots vanquishing bittersweet and other invasive weeds. When the pile of cuttings stood high enough, he'd set it aflame. She'd go down to stand beside him in the field while he presided with a rake.

"Miss Cutting! What did I say?" Sally Parks was suddenly beneath her in the hall, flapping her hands. "Please go back up and stay in your room. There's nothing you can do. I've called for help. The trucks will be here any minute." She rushed off toward the kitchen.

Henrietta continued to descend the stairs. She went through the front hall into the dining room, crossed to the windows, and there witnessed an extraordinary sight. The garage was in flames! Red-hot tongues of fire were licking the walls. Rolling clouds of smoke swirled up past the eaves.

Her first thought was for the girls. They'd been in and out of the building for weeks, carrying wood and tools down to the raft. Henrietta's heart gave a jump of fright. Oh dear, oh dear! Were they trapped inside?

Then she remembered that she'd just seen the pond girl on the raft, miles away, water on all sides. The other, the nervous follower, would not be here alone.

Henrietta pulled a chair over from the long mahogany table (once the site of her parents' famous dinner parties) and seated herself in comfort before the windows. Directly in front of her the fire roared and crackled.

Two fire trucks arrived with shrieking sirens. Men in black rubber jumped out. They hauled hoses from the trucks and commenced spraying. A third truck arrived. Then a fourth! Fountains of water pounded into the fiery cauldron.

Off to the side Henrietta spotted Sally Parks in an old yellow sailing slicker—of all things! She must have borrowed it from the back hall closet. The woman was running around like a barnyard hen giving orders, as she always did. Useless in this instance. The flames would not obey. They leaped ever higher until the whole garage was engulfed. The roof collapsed. Windows popped out. Gutters melted, trellises fell, and . . . with no effort at all Henrietta finds herself floating up through the smoky air and whisking down to the pond.

She arrives on the raft and begins to look at the flames from her new vantage. Suddenly it seems to her that it isn't just the garage that's burning, it's everything up there. It's the whole blessed house! Porches, dormers, kitchen wing, solarium, bedrooms, bathrooms. A breathtaking spectacle!

Like a fire in heaven.

Henrietta has her raft pole in hand. She's about to thrust it into the water and begin her departure. She's decided to go on, to start a new life on the other side of the pond with the gray foxes. It's a good time to leave. Everyone is riveted by the fire. *No one will miss me!*

"Miss Cutting! What are you doing down here!"

Henrietta turned with a jerk. She seemed to have dozed off in her chair. Her mind had wandered away. Now it snapped back into place and there she was in the dining room again, face-to-face with Sally Parks. Some time had passed because the garage outside, while still burning, was not so bright as before. The fire brigade was successfully containing it, though a large amount of smoke was still pouring out.

"Oh dear, I'm afraid Father's workshop is done for," Henrietta murmured, embarrassed to be caught napping.

Sally shook her head. "Not at all. We've saved a good portion of the back. That part will survive."

"Father would be so pleased."

She was taken back upstairs, fed a tuna fish sandwich and milk, and settled once again in her chair by the window while Sally returned to oversee the final act below.

It was then that Henrietta caught sight of the pond girl again. She'd returned from the bog and was standing on the raft in the middle of the pond. She was staring at the fire with fixed concentration, the same way Henrietta had watched it in her recent hallucination.

For a moment Henrietta's mind slips again and she is standing beside the girl on the raft. Together they watch the garage burn on shore. Henrietta feels a powerful bond rise between them, a burst of recognition that they are one and the same, kindred souls whose lives have intersected and merged.

It doesn't last, because abruptly the girl steps away from

her and goes into action. She plants the pole on the muddy bottom and begins to take the raft swiftly up the pond. She comes to the overgrown spit of sand that reaches out like an arm into the water, rounds the bend, and disappears.

The pond girl disappears and leaves Henrietta behind. She leaves her trapped at the window, alone in the world, pressing a pair of binoculars hard against her watery eyes.

NINETEEN

"Did you hear about the big fire?" Julia asked that evening at dinner.

Jonathan sat up. "Where!"

"At the Cutting house. The garage caught on fire. You could see the smoke from the beach."

"I thought I smelled smoke," their father said. "Late this afternoon I kept thinking I smelled it."

"What happened? What happened!" Jonathan bounced in his chair.

"Well, it burned, I suppose," Julia said. "Somebody said fire departments from three towns were called in."

"Does anyone know how it started?" Richard Kettel laid a calming hand on his son.

"Can we go see it, Dad? Tonight! Right now!"

"It's probably mostly out by now. What time was it when you saw it at the beach, Julia?"

"Around four, I think."

"So it's out," he told Jonathan. "You can sit back down."

Jessie had stopped eating. She had put her hand over her mouth.

"What's the matter?" her father asked.

"Nothing."

"Maybe I'll find out more tonight," Julia went on. "Apparently, the police were called in too. Like maybe it was foul play."

"What's foul play?" Jonathan asked her.

"It's when something isn't right, like the fire was started by unnatural means. Like some person did it. On purpose."

Jessie rose from the table and left the kitchen.

"Are you all right?" her father called.

"I'm just going to look," she called back. "I'm just going to see if you can still see it."

"I am too!" Jonathan yelled. He pounded up the stairs behind her. In their room at the end of the hall, they stood at the windows and looked up the pond. A muted glow came through the trees.

"Is that it?" Jonathan asked.

"I think so."

"Can you see any fire trucks?"

"No."

"I guess it's mostly out, then."

"I hope it's out."

"Did the garage burn all the way down, do you think?"

"I don't know."

"Do you think it's foul play?"

"I don't know."

"I bet it's foul play," Jonathan said, "otherwise why would the police have come?"

"I don't know." Jessie's hand had gone up over her mouth again.

That night, long after Jonathan had gone to bed and her father had retired, Jessie stayed downstairs in the living room, assaulted by dark thoughts.

The fire would bring on an investigation. The police would come to check the scene. They'd want to know what had started the blaze, what was in the garage, who might have been in there recently, who might have had access.

If the garage had burned all the way down, there would be no evidence of a break-in. There would be no sign of what had been stolen by the robbers, or of the tools Terri had returned. What there would be was a trail that led down to the pond. There'd be signs of activity on the shore. There might even be footprints in the mud. Hers. And Terri's, of course.

Jessie was hunched down on the couch, listening to the pond and feeling the raw creep of danger, when Julia came in, half an hour late. Her hair was in a tangle and her chamois shirt was buttoned up the wrong way.

"Hi," Julia said loudly. "What's wrong?"

"Nothing."

"Why are you still up?"

"Because I am. Is that a problem?"

"No."

"What was going on out there? You sat in the car for about an hour."

"Nothing was going on. We were just talking."

"Really! Who with?"

"None of your business."

"Was it Ripley Schute?"

"Why do you care?"

"Well, was it?"

"Yes." Julia smoothed her hair and went toward the kitchen. "I'm making tea," she said. "Do you want some?"

"No." Jessie followed her and hung in the kitchen doorway. She watched her sister put on the kettle and take a mug from the cabinet.

"Why are you watching me?"

"I'm not!"

"Well, what's the matter, then?" Julia gave her an angry look. It changed suddenly to concern. "Hey, are you okay? Are you in some kind of trouble? Tell me. What is it?"

Jessie shook her head. "It isn't me. It's you. I heard something you might want to know."

Julia snorted and tore open a packet of tea.

"Don't get mad. I really think you should know."

"Know what?"

"About Ripley Schute. He's a creep. He got somebody in trouble last summer."

"Who said?"

"Terri told me. She knows about things like that."

"Oh, Terri! It was probably her."

"No. She was just nice enough to tell me."

"I thought you stopped hanging out with her."

"I have."

"Well, good!"

"Julia, listen. A lot of people know about Rip, they just aren't telling you. Because he's part of their crowd and his family has money. He's a con artist. He picks on girls who just got here, who don't know anything."

"Well, thanks. You can go to bed now," Julia snapped. "You stayed up all this time to inform me of this important fact?"

"No."

"Yes, you did. You could hardly wait to tell me."

"Julia—"

"Leave me alone!" Julia exploded. "You don't know what you're talking about!"

She walked furiously out the back door into the night, where she waited for Jessie to go upstairs before coming back in.

In the dark of her room Jessie stood at the window and looked out toward the Cuttings' house again. A faint glow was still visible there, a rustle of movement. Perhaps a fire engine was still at the scene. Or was a policeman already poking around for clues?

She hoped the garage had burned to the ground. If it had, there'd be less chance that the looting and robberies would be discovered, and no reason to investigate a crime that might lead back to her and Terri. At least the tools weren't still down on the shore. She thought of how Terri had put them back, taking the risk of running into trouble so Jessie wouldn't have to worry. So they could be friends again.

Friends. If it was hard before, it was impossible now. Things had gone way too far. Poor Terri. Whatever way she turned, life worked against her. No matter how awesome she was determined to be, no matter how much she wanted to get out and start over, it was already too late. She'd never do it. She'd never win. How maddening it must be to find yourself always on the losing side. So maddening that you might even . . .

A terrible thought weaseled its way into Jessie's mind. Standing at the window, with Jonathan asleep in his bed behind her, she remembered Terri's fire wand. She saw Terri flick it on with a smile of triumph.

"Pretty cool, right?" she heard her say. "You can light anything with this."

TWENTY

There was nothing Jessie could do but wait and pretend.

Pretend that the fire at the Cuttings' was no business of hers. Pretend that she was mildly interested when she heard that part of the garage had been saved. Pretend to be shocked when arson was said to be the cause. Pretend not to care that the Carrs were under investigation. Naturally, they would be, since they'd gotten away before with burning down a whole barn. (Julia said this.)

Pretend not to be wondering all the time about Terri and what was happening to her.

What was happening began to leak out toward the end of the week. Jessie heard it from Julia, who heard it from her group at the beach. Their father heard it from the helpful desk clerk at the library. Even Jonathan heard it. Philip's mother talked about "a child out of control" to her friend at the pool.

Terri was being questioned.

"They found a kind of camp she made down on the pond," Jessie's father said, looking at her.

"Sure. I told you about it," Jessie said.

"She'd been making fires there."

"She was living there. She had a campfire for cooking. She couldn't go home, remember?"

"They found lighter fluid. A can half-full."

"Well, she'd been using it to light her fires!"

"They think lighter fluid was used to start the Cutting fire."

"Anybody can buy lighter fluid, Dad! Half the people here have it for their outdoor grills."

The authorities hadn't yet discovered the fire wand, because the next thing her father said was:

"They found a whole box of wooden matches at Terri's camp. Jessie, could she have done this? Set this fire?"

"No!" Jessie said. "Terri wouldn't do that. She's basically a good person."

It wasn't easy to say that, knowing what she did. Or to keep on saying it with Julia around always thinking the worst. Being happy to think the worst, as if the depths of Terri's nature had been confirmed. As if she were depraved, beyond help, an apple rotten to the core.

"That kid's been heading down the drain for a long time," Julia said.

"And how would you know?" Jessie demanded. "You've only been here a month. You never knew her before that."

"I heard about her. If you really want to know, I could tell by looking at her."

"Julia!"

"It's true."

"So what was it, her cutoffs or her flip-flops? Was it her hair or her face or her feet that told you?"

"All of that," Julia said. "She never looked clean. And she had a sneaky expression. And her teeth are brown."

"Julia, I think you're going a little overboard on appearances," their father said. "None of that makes someone a criminal. I think you're judging too harshly."

"Just wait," Julia said. "You'll see I'm right. People who look a certain way are usually what you think they are. Where there's smoke there's fire. Especially in Terri's case."

The Kettel family had ten days left of their East Coast vacation when Terri's smoke began to drift down to their end of the pond. It arrived at the front door in the shape of a local policeman, the same shirtsleeved officer Jonathan and his father had encountered up at the station when they went to report the stolen laptop.

"Hello, sir. I'm Sergeant Jared Smith. Nice to see you again. How's that little son of yours?"

"He's fine. Off swimming at a neighbor's house."

"It's certainly a good day for a swim. Hot as blazes! Sorry to bother you, sir. The reason I'm here is we're following up on a report that some kids were seen on a raft out there on the pond. . . . Yes, in the last month or so. We know you've been renting here for about that long, and we wondered . . . I see. Your daughter? Well, it's probably nothing, but would it be possible for me to ask her a few questions? We've had a terrific fire up at the Cutting residence, don't know if you've heard about it. We believe it may have been purposely set. Perhaps your daughter could shed some light on the case. Her name is . . . ?"

Jessie listened to this conversation with a galloping heart from the upstairs hall. She expected her father to call her down, already had one foot on the top stair when she heard him say:

"Jessica is out at the moment. At the beach with her sister, I think. What sort of thing did you want to ask her?"

"Mainly about Teresa Carr. Terri, she's called. Do you happen to know if she's a friend of your daughter's?"

With amazement, Jessie listened to her father's answer.

"A friend? No, I wouldn't say so. I believe they've met. My daughter did find a raft when we first moved in here. Just bobbing in the pond. She's spent some time on it, but from what I understand, the Carr girl has it now. She more or less took it over. Jessica hasn't been on it recently, I know."

"Well, that's about what we figured."

"Has there been some trouble with Terri, I mean Teresa? She's from a family that lives down at the end of the pond, isn't she?"

"The Carrs. Yes. There's some thought she may have been involved with the fire. We have her in custody now."

"She's in *jail*?"

"Not jail. She's just a kid. The correctional center up in Canville. You know, for juveniles. She's there temporarily while we get an understanding of what went on. She hadn't been home for several days when we found her. She's been in trouble on and off in the past. The family's pretty dysfunctional."

"I see. I see."

"Mr. Kettel, I'd appreciate it if you'd ask your daughter when she comes in about her relationship with Terri, if there was one. There are signs that this raft might've been going in there at the Cuttings'. We think it might've been a landing spot Terri was using. There's some indication the garage was broken into before the fire started."

"Well, my goodness. That's terrible. I'll certainly ask her. I don't think she'll know much. She hasn't spoken about anything like that."

"No, I'm sure not. It's not the kind of situation she'd be likely to get in. But give me a call, if you would, one way or the other."

Jessie sat down on the top step while her father walked the officer out to his car. She was still sitting there when he came back in and shouted: "Jessica Kettel!"

"Dad, I'm here."

He appeared below her with a horrified face.

"Dad, I was here the whole time. You know, I *was* friends with Terri. You didn't have to lie about it. And you didn't have to pretend that you didn't know the Carrs."

He came up the stairs and stood before her. "Jessie, my Lord! Were you and Terri at the Cuttings'? Were you taking the raft in there?"

"We were," she said. "A lot of times. That's where we were fixing it up."

"But why? Why there, of all places?"

"We were borrowing tools from the Cuttings' garage. There's an old workshop in it. Or there was until it burned. We didn't take anything."

Richard Kettel ran his hands through his hair.

"I need to hear the whole story. Beginning to end, the whole blasted story of what you've been doing since we got here. Do you realize you're on the edge of being dragged into something serious? Do you know how close you just came?"

Jessie followed him to the kitchen, where he made himself a double espresso, or perhaps it was a triple, while she explained everything. Including how Henrietta Cutting had come down from her mansion and more or less invited them to use the tools.

"Did she actually say that? 'You can use my tools'?"

"No, but . . ."

Her father groaned.

She told how someone, maybe Terri's brothers but maybe someone else—"There's a lot of drug use around here, you know, Dad"—began to break into the garage and steal things. How she and Terri couldn't bring the tools back right away because of that, but Terri did return them eventually.

"Terri returned them or Terri *said* she returned them?" her father wanted to know.

"She told me she did."

"I see. And you believed her?"

"Yes! You know, you could've let me say all this to the

policeman. You didn't have to pretend I wasn't here. Why did you even do that? We didn't do anything wrong. I would've just told the truth."

But her father, who'd finished his coffee and was alternately shaking his head and holding it in his hands, said: "I'd better call your mother."

"Why?"

"She's a lawyer. She'll know what to tell the police. We're going to have to handle this carefully."

"But why?"

"Because the truth might not be enough. Not with Terri saying God knows what about you. She must've told them already that you were out there with her, landing at the Cuttings'. That's why the police were here. Who knows what else she'll say? She might even blame you."

"She wouldn't do that."

"How do you know?"

"I know her, Dad. She's a good person."

Her father sprang up and went for the telephone in the living room. "Don't you go anywhere!" he bellowed. "From now on, you're staying right here in this house. I'm calling your mother!"

It was amazing how fast she came. Jessie had thought of her as disconnected, unreachable, hundreds of miles and many hours away. She'd forgotten how swiftly her mother could move when trouble threatened. By noon the next day she'd arrived (via air) and been delivered (via taxi) and gotten settled into Julia's room. In Julia's bed, actually. Julia moved in with Jessie and Jonathan, taking over Jonathan's bed while he was relocated to cushions on the floor and a sleeping bag borrowed from Philip's family.

"This is the best!" he shouted, trying it out the first time. "This is the way I always *wanted* to sleep."

"You are like the old-time Japanese," his mother told him. "They slept on the floor with their heads on blocks of wood."

"Well, where's my wood?"

"You are a modern American boy, so you have a pillow."

Jonathan gazed at her with adoring eyes. He was the one who'd truly missed her. The others smiled at her carefully. Julia, dislodged from her room, hoped that at least her midnight curfew wouldn't be downgraded to eleven thirty. Richard worried that the house, whose dim lights and peaceful evenings he'd come to cherish, would bore her. Jessie, expecting to be grilled at any moment, watched her mother sponge off the sticky kitchen counters and purse her lips at the washing machine.

"We aren't doing our laundry here," Jessie informed her. "Dad takes it up the road to a Laundromat. Then we all fold our own when he brings it back."

"Jonathan folds his own clothes?"

"Well, we help him," Jessie admitted.

She was not grilled. Not right away. She was hugged, and her bangs were ruffled back from her forehead. She was told how blond she'd become, how browned and freckled by the sun, how much taller she seemed. And how quiet.

"Has she been this quiet all summer?" Jessie heard her mother ask her father in a moment when they thought they were alone.

"No. I don't think so."

"Is she depressed, do you think?"

"Why would she be?"

"Well, that friend. Terri. What do you think was going on?"

"Nothing, as far as I can tell. They were hanging out on the pond, on that raft. They were using an old clothesline prop for a pole. Jessie found it in the backyard."

"This backyard?" Marilyn Kettel asked, glancing outside. "Does anyone ever come to cut the grass?"

"Not that I know of," Jessie's father replied. "I'm afraid there's no wireless connection either, or cell service. I go up to the library when I need to connect. That's where I found out about . . ." His voice dropped to a level Jessie couldn't hear.

"Tell me about Terri's family," Jessie heard her mother say. But then, as if they knew she was listening, the kitchen door was firmly closed.

They all went out to dinner the first night, to a local tavern. Also the second; Chinese this time. They took sandwiches to the beach, swam, and ate lunch together on their towels. They shopped for food, all five of them, at a big supermarket out of town. They went to the whaling museum in New Bedford and played a hilarious game of Animal, Vegetable, Celebrity on the way home. (Jonathan, in league with Julia, won with Snoop Dogg.)

Julia came in at ten p.m. without anyone telling her to. Jonathan said he was tired of Philip and gave up the pool. Their father asked their mother in a kind voice how the law firm was faring without her, to which she gently responded, "Let's not think about that." She didn't mention water pollution once. The kitchen was "a darling little nook." Swimming in the ocean was perfectly adequate for staying clean, she announced. Who needed a shower, rusty, trickling, or otherwise? It was the worst kind of excess! (Recognizing himself, Richard Kettel erupted in laughter.)

She bought everyone flip-flops and summer hats and caps. She took photos of them together against backdrops of coastal beauty. In the space of three days Jessie's mother charmed her husband and drew her children around her. She brought them out of their corners and united them into the kind of family other people smiled at in restaurants. She made them laugh and she made them impregnable.

Then: "Jessie," she said, pulling her daughter aside at last. "There's something we need to discuss."

By this time the story of Terri Carr and the fire at the Cuttings' garage had gone the rounds. New evidence was being examined by the police. A single flip-flop had been found floating in the pond near the Cuttings' landing. A tube of first-aid cream had been left in the bushes. Muddy footprints had been discovered in the garage workshop, the only section that had escaped damage from the fire.

The Kettels had been contacted again by Sergeant Jared Smith. This time he requested a formal interview with Jessie.

It was now clear that she and Terri had been something more than just acquaintances. Their month-long connection was known at the beach, where a member of the Kettel family had spoken of it to her friends. ("Oh, I'm so sorry!" Julia exclaimed. "I hope I haven't gotten you in trouble!")

"Jessie," her mother said. "We need to talk. Let's go shopping."

They drove out of town to the highway, up the highway to a mall.

"A little seedy, but there's a Macy's. I'll bet we can find you some new things for school."

Jessie nodded.

"You used to love to go shopping. Don't you anymore?"

"I still do. I just can't think what I need."

"Shoes?" her mother asked. "A new pair of boots?"

"I guess."

"A nice winter jacket. Or a hoodie?"

"Mom."

"How about one of those suede vests everyone's wearing now?"

"Mom."

"I'll try one on too. I've always wanted something with fringe."

"Mother!" Jessie burst into tears.

Suddenly they were crying and hugging in the front seat, in the middle of the mall parking lot. Cars arrived and departed around them, drivers pretending to ignore their teary drama.

"I am so sorry, sweetie! I can see you're tied up in knots over this whole situation," her mother said, offering a tissue.

"I am!" Jessie wept. "I don't know what to do. Terri's such a great person. If you knew her, you'd see. She tries so hard. It's completely unfair that they sent her to that place for juvenile delinquents."

"I'm sure it is," her mother sympathized. "I'm sure she's wonderful."

"She really is! It's not her fault."

"I'm sure she has terrible trouble at home."

"Oh, she does. They don't have any money. She has to steal from her father when she needs some. And he beats her up."

"Oh dear!"

"At school they look down on her. The whole town looks down on her family. Somebody poisoned her cat."

"No!"

"Yes, they did. He died."

"Terrible! But what do you really think, could Terri have set that fire?" Marilyn Kettel asked, getting down to brass tacks.

"No!"

"Did she steal our laptop?"

"I don't think so."

"Did she know the Cuttings' garage was being burgled and trashed?"

"Maybe. I don't know."

"By her own brothers? Didn't you tell Dad she said that? So wouldn't she have known?"

Jessie was silent. She thought of the pretty china in the box that Terri had admired.

"All right, we don't know that for sure," her mother went on. "But we know quite a lot about Terri otherwise, don't we? We know she's used to living on the edge of the law."

"She has a knife," Jessie said.

"A knife?"

"A switchblade. It's for protection. She said if someone came at her in the dark, she could kill them."

"Oh my."

"She got suspended from school for having it. After a fight with another girl."

"Hmmm."

"People are always accusing her family of bad things. It started when her great-grandfather went to prison for life. For murder."

Her mother sighed.

"Terri said he didn't do it. She said he was framed."

"Do you think he was?"

"I don't know."

They were both silent. Finally Jessie said in a hesitant voice, "Mom, Terri had a fire wand. A thing for starting fires."

"What?"

"She said it was for her campfire, when she was living outside. I've been thinking of it ever since the Cuttings' garage went up. She was really upset that I didn't want to see her anymore. She thought she'd made us friends again by taking back the tools. That was the afternoon the fire broke out. It might be my fault."

"Your fault? How ridiculous!" her mother exclaimed. "If there's one thing I'm sure of it's that this has nothing to do with you!"

Through the windshield the scorched wasteland of the mall parking lot spread before them. A young mother walked past, shepherding her three small children, keeping a fierce eye out for oncoming cars.

Marilyn Kettel stiffened in her seat.

"Now, Jessie," she began. "We need to talk about the conversation you'll be having with the police. They'll want to know all sorts of things. You must be very careful what you say. Your father and I will be there, of course. We'll be ready to help you."

They spent the drive home going over the details of what Jessie should say. How she must tell the absolute truth of what she knew and didn't know. For instance, that she didn't know they weren't allowed in the garage. She thought they had permission to use the tools.

"Should I bring Miss Cutting into it?" Jessie asked.

"I wouldn't. Just say, clearly, that you thought you had permission. Didn't Terri's father used to work for the Cuttings? There's your answer."

"Do I have to tell about the fire wand? I'm not really sure about it."

"I think you should. And you must make it absolutely clear that the friendship had broken down by then. You were worried, you must say, about where Terri was leading you. You can mention the laptop, but I wouldn't get into the thefts in the garage. That brings you a little too close."

Jessie nodded.

"Do you see where I'm headed with this?" her mother asked. "You must tell the truth, but in such a way that you cannot be accused of being involved."

"What about Terri?" Jessie asked.

"Terri must take care of herself," her mother replied.

TWENTY-ONE

The morning of Jessie's interview with the police dawned a warm summer blue. A clannish murmuring of Canada geese came from the pond. Overhead, out of sight, a small plane's sleepy drone rose on a coastal breeze and faded peacefully over the horizon.

There was no peace inside the Kettel cottage. The whole family had been jolted awake by a travel alarm at six forty-five. By seven thirty breakfast was being served. By eight o'clock Jonathan was being outfitted for the beach and Julia was at the sink washing dishes. Jessie had been sent upstairs a second time to change her clothes.

"And comb your hair more neatly," Marilyn Kettel called after her. "You need to leave a good impression." She herself was wearing a silk blouse, a pencil skirt, and dark city pumps.

"Are you going back to work?" Jonathan asked her anxiously.

At eight fifteen Richard Kettel, in a clean white shirt and jacket, went out to make sure the car would start. The salt air was taking a toll on the belts. A high whine set in whenever he turned on the ignition, and the engine tended to cough. How glad he would be, he announced, to get back to a climate (Pittsburgh) he knew and understood.

By eight thirty everyone was in the living room, congregated around Jessie.

"How do you feel?" her father asked.

"I feel fine."

"There's nothing to be nervous about," her mother said.

"I know."

"You look nervous," Julia said.

"Oh, thanks."

"Do you have a pretty good idea of what to say?" her father asked.

"Yes."

"We've been over it," her mother said. "She just has to tell the truth. The police are on our side. They'll give us the benefit of the doubt."

"*Is* there any doubt?" Julia inquired. "I thought everything was pretty clear."

"It is," her mother said.

"Why can't I go?" Jonathan complained.

"Because you'd be bored," his mother told him. She pulled his sagging swim trunks up around his waist and tied the string in front more tightly. "You and Julia are going to have a lovely morning at the beach."

Julia sighed. "At least you could drop us off in the parking lot. What's the big rush?"

"No rush. We just want to be on time. Somebody will

probably pick you up on the way," her mother said. "People are so friendly around here."

"Time to be off!" her father exclaimed.

They all walked stiffly to the car, where Jessie got in the backseat and her parents got in the front. They waved good-bye, leaving Julia and Jonathan plodding up the long drive-way.

They drove most of the way in weighty silence. But as they approached the station in the center of town, Jessie's mother turned around and said:

"Smile."

"What?"

"Right now. Give me a smile. . . . Good. I just wanted to be sure you didn't have any leftover cereal in your teeth."

"Mom!"

"You don't."

Jessie hadn't expected to see Terri at the police station. She'd assumed she was still at the correctional center in Canville. Suddenly there she was, coming out the station door just as the Kettels were going in.

"Hi," Jessie said. "Are you back home now?"

Terri shrugged. "I don't know yet."

It was all they had time for, they passed so quickly. Jessie might not have even noticed the odd position of Terri's arms, the flash of metal at her waist, if she hadn't been looking at her clothes. She had on a collarless lime-green shirt that Jessie had never seen before, and matching cotton pants that looked like pajamas. More shocking than that, her dark hair had been cut off as short as a boy's. A woman official steered her through the door. Behind them both strode Mitch Carr with an angry look on his face. Jessie's father stepped aside without speaking to let him pass.

Jessie's mother put her arm firmly around Jessie's shoulders so she couldn't look back.

"Were they interviewing Terri this morning too?" Jessie asked.

"I have no idea," her mother answered.

"She was wearing handcuffs."

Her mother didn't answer. She marched Jessie straight ahead.

The interview was conducted in a small room without windows. Jessie sat on a couch between her parents. Sergeant Smith was behind a desk, friendly and apologetic.

"So sorry to drag you in here in the middle of your vacation. I won't keep you long. I just want to tie up a few loose ends."

He looked at Jessie.

"So you're the one who found the raft," he said with a grin. "Must've been left over from last summer. Or maybe the summer before. That saltbox you're in doesn't always rent out. Too primitive for some."

"I found it floating near the bank of the pond," Jessie said. "It was waterlogged."

"Then you ran into Terri where, near your house?"

"It was near her house. I'd found a pole and took the raft up the pond. She came out and got on it with me."

"And that was the first time you met?"

"Yes."

"After that, who kept the raft?"

"In the beginning I did mostly, on the bank near our house. Terri came over in the mornings and we'd take it on the pond."

"Terri wouldn't come in," her father interjected. "She'd sit outside in the grass and wait for Jessie to come out."

"Did that seem unusual?" Sergeant Smith asked.

"No," Jessie said at the same time her father answered, "A little."

"Well, it worried our older daughter," her father explained. "She'd heard some things on the beach about Terri. And then our laptop was stolen."

"That was later," Jessie objected, but Sergeant Smith held up a hand.

"Just a moment. What kinds of things had your older daughter heard? What's her name?"

"Julia," Richard and Marilyn Kettel answered together.

"She'd heard that Terri had been in trouble for shoplifting," Jessie's father said. "And about the kind of family she came from. I began to realize she was, you know, disadvantaged."

"But that was much later, Dad," Jessie protested again. "In the beginning you liked Terri. You said she seemed like a nice person."

The officer was writing something on a pad and didn't look up. Jessie's father went on as if he hadn't heard her.

"From what we understand, Terri took our daughter up to

a house where there was a tool workshop of some kind. The idea was to fix up the raft, make it float better."

"That's where I was going next," Sergeant Smith said. He looked at Jessie. "Did you take tools from the Cuttings' garage?"

"We only meant to borrow them," Jessie said. "They were in an old workshop in the garage where no one had been for years. We brought some down to the raft so we could fix it. We weren't stealing."

"Jessie told us she thought she had permission to use the tools," her mother said.

Jessie nodded. "I did sort of think that because—"

"Terri had said her father worked for the Cuttings," her mother interrupted, "so naturally Jessie assumed it was all right to borrow the tools."

"Is that right, Jessie?" the officer asked.

Jessie shifted in her chair. "Well, sort of," she said. "It was kind of a fine line. I went along with it because Terri thought it was okay."

Sergeant Smith nodded. "I understand. I guess Terri was shading the truth a little. Mitch Carr once did some groundskeeping for the Cuttings, but that was over long ago. There was nothing that would've entitled her to be in their garage. But let's go on. Did you put the tools back after you were through with them?"

"Not right then," Jessie said. "Because someone had started breaking into the garage and we were afraid to go back. Terri said we should wait and not get involved."

"Did you get the idea that she might know who was breaking in?"

"I don't think she knew for sure. She said there were people around who might be doing it because they were, you know, addicts. Or they might have just been hard up."

"So she wasn't too surprised that it was happening?"

"I don't know if she was surprised, but she was worried," Jessie said.

"Worried that it might be discovered?"

"No. Just that it was happening."

Sergeant Smith put down his pencil. "And after that?"

"Well, I got scared," Jessie said. "I could see how things were getting out of control. So that's when I asked Terri to take me home. I said she could have the raft."

"So the friendship broke up?"

Jessie's mother leaned forward. "I wouldn't call it a 'friendship' in the normal sense of the word," she said. "Terri offered a way to fix Jessie's raft, that's all. It's not as if our family knew the Carrs or they knew us. Jessie was never in their house and Terri was never in ours. By invitation, at least. They never went to the movies together or to the beach. It was a relationship of convenience more than anything. The moment Jessie saw where she was being led, she stopped. Isn't that right, sweetie?"

Jessie looked down. "Sort of. We really were friends, though." She turned to her mother. "It wasn't convenience. I really liked Terri and she liked me."

"Well, then, tell the officer about Terri's fire starter," her mother said.

"Oh, we already know about the lighter fluid at her camp," Sergeant Smith said. "Terri says she was using it to start her own campfires."

"No, this is different. Jessie, tell what you saw. Tell what it made you think about the fire."

Jessie couldn't answer right away. A sick feeling was welling up inside her. She didn't want to say what they wanted her to say, but she was afraid to go against them too. She twisted in her chair and thought how miserable Terri had looked going out the station door, her hands linked together, her hair cut off, wearing clothes that weren't hers, without anyone to help her. There was only Mitch, looking mean and disgusted, and the woman officer guiding her through the door, holding fast to her arm. As if Terri were dangerous or might try to get away. As if nobody trusted her for one minute, anywhere.

"Jessie?"

Sergeant Smith had stepped out around his desk. He was drawing a chair up directly opposite her. He sat down and leaned forward so she couldn't avoid his eyes.

"Jessie, I'd appreciate you telling me what you saw," he said. "It will help us to know more about the whole situation, and it will help Terri, too. She's been at risk for some time. You and your parents are newcomers here, understandably unaware of her past. To state it plainly, Terri Carr isn't headed in the right direction. She's headed into trouble. You'd be doing her a favor to tell us what you know. You'd be acting like a friend."

TWENTY-TWO

If it hadn't been for the raft, Henrietta Cutting would never have known who the killers were. They would have been just men in gray coats and wet boots, standing in the front hall below her; men with guns.

As silent and quick as a shoal of silvery minnows, the raft could slip between shadowed reeds. It could creep up the shore like an invisible wind, barely disturbing the water. She was on a mission that day, in the summer of her twelfth year, to find the snapper. Over a century old, it was said to be, though no one she knew had actually seen the great turtle. Did it exist? Was it a fact or a fiction? Henrietta was determined to find out. Sunbathing was a snapper habit, she'd read. That morning she was out early, canvassing the mud flats and the boggy edges around the pond, hoping to catch the enormous creature asleep on a bank.

What she caught instead were words of a hushed conversation coming through the reeds.

"Cooper, what kind of pistol is that?"

"A Browning semiautomatic. Brand new."

"Very pretty. Very pretty. You're not going to shoot out here with it, are you?"

"Not here. It's for later. The big man said we're to give it back after."

"That's the way these days. You can't even keep your own piece."

"We'll be cleaning up in other ways, so what's the difference? Shhh. I heard something."

Henrietta crouched on the raft and waited.

"Thought I heard a wood duck," said the hunter named Cooper. He had a high, hoarse voice.

"Could've been a loon."

"Nah. Not this far south."

"Well, I don't see a thing around here right now," a third man complained. "How about we go farther up so Buster and me can get a look at the terrain."

"We haven't been out here a half hour and Shootsy's already getting antsy," the Cooper voice said with a scratchy chuckle. "Sure, let's go. Let's give Shootsy a look around."

"Just for the record, I do my work with my own piece," Shootsy growled. "A good old shotgun. Hey, anyone got a light? I could use one."

There was the scrape of a match. The smell of cigarette smoke drifted through the reeds. Henrietta lay down flat as the three passed within six feet in a rowboat and headed out into the pond.

She guessed the man named Cooper was Albert's father.

He didn't visit the family cabin often enough to be familiar, but she saw a resemblance. And she saw his hunting companions, brawny men with ball-game caps and open-necked shirts.

Mr. Cooper, on the oars, wore a hat and tie. He had reddish hair and a pink complexion like his son, now verging on tomato. All three men looked overheated, though it was still quite early in the day. Inexperienced hunters, Henrietta thought they were. She watched them go up the pond until their voices faded and she was sure she could move the raft undetected. She resumed her own hunt for the snapper, a will-o'-the-wisp she never did encounter.

She recognized them that night. Those three hunters were the men in the hall with her mother and father. But at the time no one ever asked her. The police had caught the killer, she was told. In her dazed state she never questioned it. She was taken to a private home near Philadelphia, where her mother's cousins lived. Then, when she was better, she was sent across to England. It wasn't until she came back years later that she understood Eddie Carr had been convicted.

"The milkman?" she said. "But he wasn't even there!"

She knew Eddie. He was a cheerful, dark-haired man of twenty-five or so who delivered their milk from his family farm down the road. How could he have been involved? Slowly it dawned on her: A mistake had been made! She began to tell people. She called her cousins to say the man in prison was not the right one. She spoke to her family lawyers. She telephoned the police, who said the case was closed. Too much time had passed. She was confused, they informed her. Her memory was unreliable.

Perhaps, but over the years she saw them, one or another of the killers, walking around town in broad daylight. Red-faced Mr. Cooper, or the big, brawny man people called Shootsy. She'd passed him, or someone who looked exactly like him, just the other day. She'd confronted him herself. *Murderer!* Someone had to say something!

In the end, she gave up trying to convince people. Eddie Carr had died, she heard, so what was the use? Only occasionally now was she tormented by dreams of that night. There was no telling what set them off. Sometimes a face or a voice reminded her; sometimes it was just a random collision of events.

This time it was the visit of two local police officers that stirred the sleeping snake of her memory.

"Sergeant Smith, how do you do? And you are? . . . Officer Wells. Please sit down. Is it too hot in here?" They were in the old solarium. "Mrs. Parks, would you kindly draw the shades for these gentlemen?"

Henrietta, showing a bit of her mother's Southern hospitality, was in the midst of a handshake when she caught sight of the gun. It was a short-barreled pistol, holstered in a black leather case on the officer's hip. The second officer had one too. This was bad enough, but when the two began asking questions about the girls, *her girls*, Henrietta wet her lips and grew wary. Nothing must interfere with them.

"I have occasionally seen a raft on the pond, but never close to my shore," she announced. "I have no idea who was aboard."

"Yes, you do," Sally Parks piped up from across the room. "You said they were girls. Two young girls."

Henrietta denied this with spirit. "I certainly never saw such a thing. It might've been boys, for all I know."

"So you did see somebody on a raft," the first gun queried. "I mean, there were two kids out there, am I correct?"

"No."

"You didn't see anyone?"

"Not anyone recognizable."

"Mrs. Cutting . . ."

"Miss Cutting. I never married. And never will," Henrietta added, free of charge. "What I would like to know is why you officers didn't come around before. Why was I never consulted?"

"You mean . . . about the fire?" the second gun asked.

"Not the fire. The murder! Now, if you were to ask me about that, I could give you a clear answer. It wasn't the milkman who did it. He was never there. It was Mr. Cooper and his hunters."

Both men looked over at Sally Parks. "Has there been a recent murder?" the first gun inquired.

"Not that I know of," Sally said.

"Who is Mr. Cooper?"

Sally waved a dismissive hand. "She gets a little lost sometimes. I'm sorry I can't help you myself, but I really wasn't paying attention. Miss Cutting was the one with the binoculars."

The two turned their attention back to Henrietta.

"Miss Cutting, we'd be grateful for anything you could tell us about a raft and the girl we believe was on it. Terri Carr is her name. She lives down at the end of the pond. We have reason to believe she was landing on your shore, possibly stealing from your garage. She may have started the fire."

"Ridiculous!" Henrietta exclaimed. "Why would she want to do that?"

"So you admit there was a girl."

Henrietta paused to consider. She was beginning to understand what the officers were after. They were looking for a milkman, trying to pin the fire on someone. As they had done once before, they were making a mistake. She cleared her throat and decided to tell the truth.

"I do remember now, there was a girl out on the pond that day of the fire."

The first gun nodded. "Just what we thought. Dark hair? Wiry build?"

"Yes."

"About twelve or thirteen? Shorts. Blue plaid shirt?"

"Yes."

The first gun glanced at the second gun, as if the case were already closed and this was all they'd need to wrap up a conviction. Henrietta rushed to set the record straight.

"That girl could not have set fire to my garage."

The first gun's eyes swerved back to her. "And why is that?"

"Because she wasn't anywhere near my landing that afternoon."

"Now, Miss Cutting, this is important. Exactly where on the pond was she? And at what time?" The second gun had taken over the questioning, homing in on her so fiercely that Henrietta felt a dark motor of fear switch on in her chest.

"Why, in the middle! She was standing on the raft, watching the fire."

"She was *watching* it?"

Henrietta nodded. "And then she went straight home. She took the raft and went home. I tried to wave, but I don't think she saw me."

"That may be true," Sally Parks confirmed. "Miss Cutting was standing at the window when I came upstairs. She was waving at something. I couldn't see what."

The second gun gave Henrietta a cool glance.

"From what you say, this girl could easily have *come from* your landing, couldn't she? She could've been *watching* the fire for the very reason that she started it."

"Oh, no!" Henrietta exclaimed. "She wasn't watching it that way. She was shocked, as shocked as anyone. I saw her face."

The first gun chuckled. "Now, Miss Cutting, even with binoculars, how could you have possibly determined that?"

"But I *did* see it!" Henrietta insisted. "And I'm quite

sure that girl is not the person you're looking for. I'm quite, quite sure because . . ."

At this moment Henrietta lost her bearings. Her mind, under stress, unmoored and cast off from the shores of the present. The scene shifted to the past and she began to tell a different story, the one she'd wanted to tell all along.

"There were three men in gray coats," she said in a trembling voice. "They came from the pond. I know because their boots were wet."

The policemen in the solarium leaned forward.

"Men from the pond?" Sally Parks exclaimed. "Why did you never tell me?"

"Did you see them, these three, go into the garage?" Sergeant Smith inquired.

"These men are the ones you should look for," Henrietta quavered. "They came to steal. They took my mother's jewelry box. I was there. I heard two of them talking. They agreed not to tell the one who wasn't there because then he'd never know. They wanted all the jewels for themselves."

"Miss Cutting, we're a little lost now. Did you hear this conversation from your window?"

Henrietta sighed. "I heard them and saw them. There were three! One man lit a cigarette just before . . ." She trailed off.

"Just before going in?" Sergeant Smith suggested. He had his pad out now and was writing things down.

"That would account for the cigarette butts we found near the garage door," the second gun said to his partner.

"Miss Cutting, what time would you say this was?" the sergeant asked. "Did you see anyone going into the garage before this? We believe the break-ins had been occurring over a period of time."

"I saw them before." Henrietta nodded. "No one ever asked me that, but I saw all three. They were rowing their boat, as if they were hunters."

"You mean, out on the pond?"

"Yes."

"It makes sense. You know what they're saying now: that a cigarette might've been the cause of the fire," the second gun said. "The place was a tinderbox. Old paint cans, newspapers, a load of dried-out antiques."

Both policemen glanced at Henrietta with new interest.

"Well, that certainly changes things."

Sally Parks was shaking her head. "I had no idea!"

"Miss Cutting, just a few more questions to clarify . . . ," Sergeant Smith is saying when Henrietta finds she can no longer hold her head up straight. A fog of exhaustion is creeping over her. She looks desperately at Sally for rescue. Shortly, the men are being escorted to the front door, where they confer out of earshot. Henrietta leans her head back in the chair, closes her eyes, and falls into a strange torpor that may or may not be sleep.

The snake uncoils and strikes.

It's after the fat-barreled gun has been fired and her mother has fallen lifeless to the rug that Henrietta's eyes are intercepted by the cold stare of the killer below. She knows him. He's the hunter called Shootsy from the rowboat.

"Hey, Cooper, we've got company," he drawls. The other two look up at her, one stepping forward to get a better view.

In that second Henrietta runs. She flies across the hall and back to her room, where she thinks briefly of hiding under the bed. Heavy footsteps are coming up the stairs, and she decides against this obvious place. She runs into her dressing room, which connects to her bathroom, which is itself connected to a sitting room on the other side. This is where she plays cards with her father on Sunday afternoons. There are cabinets there for storing games, the bridge table her mother uses when the ladies come, the Victrola (her mother's old-fashioned word) and its racks of records.

"Little girl, come back here. We'd like to speak to you." Mr. Cooper's scratchy voice. Henrietta recognizes it from the pond. He's reached the top of the stairs. The full glare of the hall's overhead light flicks on suddenly.

"Where did the little princess go?" Shootsy's slow voice says, heavy with sarcasm. He's closer than Mr. Cooper. He's already in her bedroom.

The sitting room, where she is, also opens onto the hall and is now partly illuminated through the door by the hall light. The sofa is too close to the floor to fit under. The cabinets are full of stuff. The curtains are three-quarter length. Her feet would show.

All three men are now upstairs, slamming around. Someone is in her dressing room, raking the wooden hangers aside. She hears the linen closet in her bathroom open and bang shut. Somebody stops to use the toilet.

"Shootsy! For God's sake."

"When you gotta go, you gotta go," Shootsy drawls, and flushes.

Henrietta uses this distraction to reenter the upstairs hall. While the hunters are tearing her bedroom apart, she slips away to her parents' room down at the end. She's begun to tremble all over, but there's no time to think of it. She almost decides to hide under the covers of her parents' big bed. She would like to be there, to curl into it and pull their blankets over her head. But she rushes past.

Her mother's dressing room is the darkest corner in the house, and smells of lavender. Her dressing table is on one side. On the other side is the door to her bathroom, where a night-light has been left on.

One of the hunters is coming down the hall.

"Little princess. Little princess," he calls, as if it's all a joke and they are playing a game of hide-and-seek. Shootsy.

From the far end of the hall, possibly the sitting room, somebody is cursing. "Where has that brat got to?"

Henrietta drops onto her knees and crawls under the flouncy fabric that skirts her mother's dressing table. She draws the little padded stool close in behind herself, turns around, and sits with her legs drawn up, her arms tight around them. Her heart is thudding in her ears and she can hear herself breathing. She puts her hand over her mouth.

Shootsy is in her parents' bedroom. He crashes into something, or throws it. A menacing quiet descends, then the scratch of a match. Henrietta sees a tiny burst of flame through the lacy cloth. He is lighting a cigarette. After a minute she smells it. Then she hears him walking around, opening her father's closets, opening drawers. He enters the dressing room, walks into the bathroom, knocks over some bottles, and comes out. The overhead light in her parents' bedroom blazes on.

"Anything here?" Mr. Cooper's voice inquires. He comes to the door of the dressing room.

"Look at this!" Shootsy says. He is standing directly in front of the dressing table. His big boots are disturbing the fabric six inches from Henrietta's eyes. The smell of his cigarette fills her nose.

"Nice jewel box. Take your pick."

"Want the ring? That is one big diamond."

"Here, let's split it up. But don't take it all. Leave some in there and take the box. We can use it."

"Right. Sure. Where's Buster?"

"He went back downstairs to look for the kid. Just put the stuff in your pocket. He'll never know."

It's while the hunters are having this conversation directly over her head, while they are pawing through the beautiful cedar jewelry box Henrietta and her father labored over for her mother, the one that nothing would ever get inside, that Henrietta half wakes into the real world. She lies still in rigid terror, unable to speak, hardly able to breathe.

Part of her realizes that the police officers and their guns have departed from the front hall. Far away in the kitchen she hears someone speaking on the telephone of daily matters in a routine voice. The hunters stir again in her mind, searching and calling for her. Which world is she in?

For a long time she balances, breathless, on the cusp.

TWENTY-THREE

O f course we're free to leave anytime," Richard Kettel was saying in the kitchen. "There's no need to stick around if we don't want to. Nothing's keeping us here."

"Yes, but the weather's so beautiful. It's so nice to be away from the office," Jessie heard her mother reply. "We can all go to the beach again. That was such fun the other day. And I was thinking, are there boats we could rent in the harbor? We might go for a sail."

"I think there are rentals available. Jonathan, would you like that?"

"I would like it if Mom came," Jonathan answered warily.

"Well, of course I'd come. That's what we're talking about. We'd all go together."

"Julia? How about you? Are you in favor of staying the rest of the week? We've paid through the nose for it, that goes without saying."

"Sure."

"And sailing?"

"Sure."

"You could bring along your friend," Jessie heard her mother say. "What's his name, Schute? He seems like a nice young man."

"I don't know if Rip'd be up for it. He's not really interested in harbor stuff."

"Is he the one who's going to Princeton this fall?" her mother asked.

"Yes."

"Well, invite him along. I'd like to get to know him."

"We should ask Jessie what she wants to do," Julia said. "She's the one who's had to deal with everything. Maybe she just wants to get out of here."

"We've *all* been dealing with things," her mother said. "Now that the problem's been settled, I, for one, would like a bit of a rest. I thought it was very poor planning by the police to have that poor girl paraded in front of us just as we were going into the station yesterday. In handcuffs, too. It certainly upset Jessie to see her. She completely forgot to say all the things we rehearsed."

"They had to get Terri's side of what happened," her father said. "They brought her down from the correctional center for the interview."

"Any other time would've been better. We all feel sorry for her, heaven knows, but when a child like that starts setting fires, you can be sure she's heading for serious trouble. Terri is following a well-trodden track. I hope she gets the help she needs before it's too late."

"But they still don't know for sure that she did it, do

they?" Jessie's father asked. "If what Jessie said is true, she wasn't anywhere near the fire that afternoon. She was over feeding some foxes across the pond."

"I don't know where that story came from," her mother said. "Jessie never told me that. And then for her to say the fire wand was broken, that Terri couldn't have used it, well, I was speechless. Luckily, in the end it didn't matter. There was no way the police were going to charge Jessie with being involved. Anyone could see the kind of family we were the minute we walked in the room. I'm so relieved we're clear of the whole thing."

"So it's agreed, then. We'll finish out the week," her father said. "Jonathan, let's you and me head down to the harbor and see if we can round up a boat. Be warned, though. Ocean sailing is a riskier enterprise than what we're used to on the lake."

"Everything is riskier with you, Dad," Julia teased. "We'll probably capsize and end up calling the coast guard."

"Well, I'm up for some of your father's good old-fashioned risk. Let the winds blow," her mother said, a smile in her voice clearly directed at her husband.

"Mom!" Julia exclaimed. "You shouldn't encourage him."

"Oh, sweetie, we're all so glad you came," Jessie's father declared with equal warmth. "You really pulled us out of a terrible mess. I don't know what would've happened if you hadn't been here."

Jessie, who'd been paused on the stairs listening to her family, turned silently and went back up. When her mother called

up later to say that she and Julia were going for a swim, she
told them to go ahead without her. When Jonathan and her
father came back from the harbor and set out again for deli
sandwiches in town, she said she'd stay home. When everyone
came back and got ready after lunch to go sailing, she told
them she needed to catch up on her summer reading.

When, at last, they were gone for good—or at least for
the rest of the afternoon—Jessie set off around the edge of
the pond. She followed the well-trodden track she and Terri
had taken together so often when they were fixing up the
raft. She followed it to Terri's camp, which was broken up
now, though the stone table was still there. If anyone had
been watching her then, they would have seen her stoop and
feel around under the table. They'd have watched her bring
out a slim, shiny object and throw it with some force far out
into the pond.

Afterward Jessie continued walking along the shore
toward the Cuttings' landing. When she got there, she went
farther. She walked on toward the Carrs'.

The pond that afternoon was in the same state of pristine
beauty as the first day of the Kettels' arrival. The green scum
from August's earlier heat wave had cleared away, leaving the
water a glittering blue. In a quiet cove a fleet of white swans
was feeding again. The sun beamed warmth from on high,
and cattails raised their curtains of privacy along the shore,
so that Jessie felt again the wild enchantment of the place
and its seclusion from all outside interference.

Except that was not quite the whole picture, she knew now. For up ahead, hidden behind a reed-infested elbow of sand, lay the Carrs' ruined home, an eyesore in the midst of loveliness, a place of menace and disorder.

She was afraid to go there, afraid to set foot on their property or, worse, to run into the Carrs themselves. She was going anyway because whatever her mother said, she couldn't end like this, by turning her back on Terri and forgetting they'd ever met.

"Protect yourself," Jessie's parents had warned, and she'd almost done it. It shocked her how close she'd come to setting Terri up, to changing the story just enough to make Terri take the blame. Even now, as she slogged toward the Carrs' house, Jessie saw how it might've been too late, how the policeman's eyes had flicked over her in disbelief.

"I know Terri didn't set that fire," she'd told him.

"And why do you think so?" he'd asked.

"Because she wouldn't do that," Jessie had answered. "When you get to know her, you know she wouldn't."

Jessie had never come so far up the pond on land. She'd seen the shoreline from the raft, but walking here was different, a change of perspective that grew more uncomfortable the nearer she came to the Carrs' property. The pond was shallower here, with fewer reeds along the edge. In some places the water shrank away from the bank, laying bare a gray and glutinous swamp. In the muck were mud-caked buoys and blackened ropes. There were empty soda cans and fast-food bags, a pink plastic doll, a rotting rowboat.

Around a bend she came across the body of a swan sprawled in a pool of sludge. It had died at a strange angle, its head crooked down upon its matted chest, one bony wing lifted up like a human arm. The story of the Peckham boys leaped into her mind. She thought how they must have cried out for help as they went down in the quicksand, and how tragic it was that no one ever answered.

She walked ahead, and soon, with no warning, the Carrs' junk-strewn yard opened in front of her. The old farmhouse was slumped at its center. She saw with relief that Mitch Carr's pickup was gone. No other vehicles were parked in the yard. It seemed at first that no one was home. But as she approached the front porch, a tiny orange kitten slid out between cinder blocks and ran mewing to meet her. Two others followed, both orange, stumbling over each other in their rush to get to her. She knelt and stroked their fuzzy heads.

"Who are you? Is anybody here?" She stood and went on toward the house, called out "Terri!" while her heart pounded like a hammer. "Hello! Anybody home?"

No answer and no movement came from inside. In an upstairs window a gray curtain flapped slowly back and forth in a breeze off the pond.

"Hello! Terri?"

She wasn't there. Jessie had guessed she wouldn't be. But now the emptiness of the house, its state of careless neglect, made a darker impression on her. Terri Carr had been taken away, sent to a place she might never come back from. Even if this was not quite true, a new dread rose inside Jessie that something very bad had happened, and that she was partly to blame.

The kittens found her again. They mewed and tried to nestle around her ankles. She bent and put her arms around all of them at once. "You poor little things." That was not what they wanted. They struggled to get loose. She let them go and began to walk around the yard.

The chicken houses Terri had built with her father were set in a hollow on one side, seven little houses with tiny windows framed by blue shutters and red window boxes. They were abandoned now, and their paint had dulled, but anyone could see they were once a labor of love.

The orange kittens caught up. They gathered around her, begging for attention.

"Where is your mother?" Jessie asked. They looked too young to be left on their own. She walked back to the house, looked under the porch where the kittens had been hiding. Two bowls were there on a roll of carpet. Farther in she saw a low wooden crate. She reached and pulled it out. The box was lined with a pink baby blanket, as fuzzy and new as the kittens themselves.

It was Terri's doing. She knew it when the kittens arrived again on her heels and came mewing under the porch to the bowls. Who else in that house would have cared what happened to them? Terri had made them this home. But she hadn't been back to feed them. The bowls were bone dry. Milk had been in one. A yellow scum was stuck to the bottom.

The kittens swarmed around her, mewing desperately.

"All right. All right!"

Jessie took the bowls and went up on the porch. When no one answered her knock, she slipped inside to a dim kitchen where a single lightbulb hung from the ceiling. She drew water into one bowl at a rusty kitchen sink. She found a nearly empty milk carton sitting out on the counter and poured what was left of it into the second bowl. She carried both bowls outside, knelt, and put them back on the carpet under the porch.

The kittens converged, falling over their own feet in their rush to drink. What would become of them if Terri didn't come back? Jessie was half tempted to scoop them up and take them home. She was considering this (would they fit in the Kettels' car?) when an engine roared in the distance. Wheels thundered toward her. Someone was coming down the dirt road that led to the Carrs' house.

Jessie ran. Whatever thoughts she'd had of making contact with Terri, or of saving the kittens, evaporated in fright. She fled toward the pond, the nearest place to hide. The driveway to the house cut directly across the path she'd walked in on. That way was fatal. She ran toward the water, out onto the dock. Mitch's old skiff floated there, tied to a post. She jumped in and hunched over between a pair of oars.

A vehicle blasted into the yard, swerved roughly on the barren lawn, braked to a stop. Someone got out and walked up the porch steps. The screen door opened with a whine and jittered shut. Jessie peered up over the dock. Mitch's pickup. He was home.

Her legs were shaking too hard to walk, much less run. She thought she might swim. She leaned over the skiff's side to look at the water and made a discovery. The raft was under the dock, nestled in shadow between the posts. Its new wooden platform floated high, just clearing the dock's underside. The poling stick was laid neatly across it.

Terri had hidden it there, Jessie knew without a doubt. She'd stowed it away for safekeeping, the same way she'd stowed the kittens under the porch. Whatever she knew about the thefts in the Cuttings' garage, whether or not she was involved with the fire there, Terri was afraid she'd be accused. She was getting ready to be taken.

The front door whined. Jessie lay down flat in the skiff, listening.

Mitch was an impatient man. She heard it in the rapid tattoo his boots made on the porch, in the irritated way he let the screen door slap shut behind him, in his dry, repetitive cough. She smelled the cigarettes he smoked as he came and went, heard him swear and kick at something that made him stumble. (One of the kittens?) He was lugging things out of the house, loading them into the truck bed. What was he doing?

Jessie raised her head just far enough to see him stagger through the door carrying a rolled-up rug over his shoulder. He teetered down the porch steps, threw the roll into the truck, and went back into the house. A minute later he reappeared with a cardboard box, set it in the truck, and returned for another. And another. A piece of newspaper escaped and blew across the lawn. He went after it, brought it back, and stuffed it into a box.

He carried out the Chinese dragon vase, then a table and some chairs. The bronze table lamp was heavier than he expected. He tripped on the steps and nearly dropped it on its stained-glass shade. When he got to the back of the truck, he shoved it between the boxes with a loud exclamation.

He went back for more, but Jessie lowered her head. She didn't need to look anymore. She wondered if he'd keep the pretty china that Terri had liked so much. Keep it for her, for his daughter. Or would he not bother now because she was gone and might not be back soon. He didn't look like a person who was thinking about that. He looked angry.

The wind was coming up the way it often did in the late afternoon near the ocean. Waves began to knock against the skiff's hull. They slammed against it harder and harder, rocked the boat side to side, until Jessie felt as if the pond would soon pour in on top of her. As the waves mounted, Jessie took from her back pocket, where she'd kept it all this time, the note she'd written Terri with her cell phone number. ("Call me in Pittsburgh. We can stay in touch! Jessie.") She slipped it onto the raft under the dock, sticking it down between the planks as best she could so it wouldn't blow away. Then she lay back in the skiff and gripped the sides with both hands.

There was nothing to do but hang on and hope that

Mitch would leave soon, that he'd finish loading his truck with the stolen goods and drive away to whatever place he planned to hide them next.

Jessie was soaking wet by the time Mitch's pickup pulled out, so cold and stiff she could hardly walk. She left the kittens behind. She hoped Terri would come home in time to save them. It was all she could do to move her feet and keep moving them along the shoreline path. She still hadn't warmed up when she reached the Kettels' end of the pond.

From a distance she saw the cottage, but the car wasn't there. The sailors hadn't yet returned from the harbor, and Jessie was glad. She needed time to recover, to put on dry clothes, quiet her mind, and get ready to join her family. She was ready to be with them again. After everything that had happened, she needed to come back. She hoped that tonight they could just be the Kettels again, on vacation together, eating dinner in the kitchen, teasing her father, laughing at one of Jonathan's hilarious remarks, recounting their adventures—except Jessie knew she would keep what she'd just seen at the Carrs' house a secret. To tell would only suck them back into the dark swamp at the end of the pond.

She was nearly at the house when a shadow moved past the screen door. A rustle came from inside. She thought it was a bird at first, something with wings fluttering through the rooms. But a moment later came a crash, and then the sound of someone running through the house. The back door slammed.

Jessie circled around back in time to see a lean figure rounding the house in the other direction, toward the driveway. By the time she got back there, the figure was pelting at top speed up the dirt road. She watched as it left the driveway and sprinted straight up the overgrown field. She watched the figure hit the main road, veer off, and run out of sight, never once looking back.

She went into the house to see what was missing.

TWENTY-FOUR

The Silent Lamb?" Julia exclaimed in astonishment. "It couldn't have been him."

"It was him," Jessie said.

"You're saying Aaron Bostwick was the one who stole Dad's laptop?"

Jessie's family stood around her, dripping with seawater. They'd just arrived from the harbor.

"I'm saying he brought it back. There it is on the table, right where it used to be. He wouldn't have brought it back for anyone else, would he?"

"But that's impossible. He's a complete straight arrow. Aaron Bostwick wouldn't steal a thumbtack. He'd be too scared."

"Maybe he's not as lambish as you think. He was pretty mad at you down at the beach, if you remember."

"When was this?" their mother asked.

Jessie filled her in while Julia stalked around the living room, saying, "I can't believe this!"

"What on earth did you do to make him so angry?" Marilyn Kettel asked her daughter.

"Nothing!" Julia exclaimed. "He gave me a few rides to the beach, and then he kept hanging around like I owed him something."

"She gave him the big brush-off," Jessie said. "He was furious. Remember how he said you'd be sorry?"

"Well." Their mother smothered a smile. "You must've hurt his feelings, Julia. It's a sensitive time in life for boys his age. This isn't the same boy as . . . what was his name who's going to Princeton?"

"Ripley Schute," Jessie said. "No, Ripley's the guy Julia moved on to afterwards. He's much cooler. His dad is rich and he has a vintage Thunderbird."

"You're insufferable," Julia hissed at her. "I haven't even seen Rip lately."

"Right, after he tried to tear your clothes off."

"He did not! That is so not true!" Julia yelled at the same time that her mother was murmuring, "My goodness. Such goings-on."

By now it was nearly six o'clock, and Jonathan's lips had turned blue from standing around in wet clothes. All the sailors were shivering. The wind had come up strongly toward the end of the afternoon, causing their sailboat to heel over in the bay.

"And Dad let go of the rope, and we went around in a circle for about an hour trying to catch it," Jonathan said accusingly.

"A slight exaggeration." Richard Kettel grasped his son's hand and began to take him upstairs. "And what is the rope

I let go of called, Jonathan? You should remember that, at least."

"The big sheet," Jonathan said.

"The *main*sheet," his father corrected him.

"Give him a bath. It'll warm him up," their mother advised. "I'll put on some dry clothes and get a start on dinner. Lobsters tonight! Aren't we the lucky ones. Have we got enough butter?"

"I think so," their father called from the top of the stairs.

The Kettels disbanded to different corners of the house to dry off and warm up and prepare for the evening. Julia gave Jessie a particularly nasty look as she went up to change.

"Traitor," she said.

"Why? It was true."

"It wasn't! Do you care at all about other people's feelings?"

"I care. A lot more than you think."

There was something else Jessie wanted to say, something that was burning her tongue to come out, but she held fire. She went into the kitchen to wait for her mother to come down so they could make dinner together, a rare treat. Not until much later, as the whole family was sitting at the kitchen table wrestling with their bright-red boiled lobsters, did Jessie bring up what was on her mind.

"So, Dad, when are you going to report the theft?" she asked.

"What theft?" he said with a full mouth.

"Of your laptop. Aren't you going to tell the police that Aaron Bostwick broke in and stole it?"

Everyone looked at her in surprise. "Why?" her father said.

"Because he did. He robbed us."

"Well, he was mad at Julia."

"Does that excuse him?"

"He brought it back," Jonathan said.

"Does that make it okay that he came in our house at night and took something? Not a thumbtack, either." She looked at Julia. "He stole a three-hundred-dollar computer."

Julia rolled her eyes. "Come on! Aaron Bostwick is hardly a criminal. He was stealing for a completely different reason. It wouldn't be fair to get him in trouble with the police."

"It wouldn't be fair to who?" Jessie asked.

"Wait. Wait. I see where you're going." Her father reached across the table and put his hand on her arm. "You're talking about Terri Carr. And you're right. We shouldn't have jumped to conclusions about her. But that was different. Everything pointed to her."

"If Terri had stolen the laptop, she wouldn't have brought it back. That's the difference," Julia said.

"And sweetie," her mother said, "Terri wasn't arrested for stealing our computer. She's charged with arson with malicious intent, which is a felony. She has a history of trouble with the law. She's just a whole other level beyond Julia's little . . . what do you call him?"

"The Silent Lamb," Jonathan informed her. "He looks more like a sheep to me."

"I don't see that," Jessie said stubbornly. "I don't see how

Terri is different. What I see is a lot of people *thinking* she's different, expecting her to do something bad, looking for a way to prove they're right. You know what? I'm going to report Aaron Bostwick to the police. I'm going to call the police right now and say I found him in our house trying to steal something else. Who knows, maybe he was. Maybe he decided the laptop wasn't enough."

"What?" they all shouted. "Are you crazy? Are you nuts?"

Jessie got up from the table, as if she really meant to do such a thing. Julia and Jonathan pulled her back down. They held her in her chair long enough for her mother to come around the table and put her arms around her and hug her. She rocked Jessie back and forth, laughing a little.

"Okay, you've made your point," her mother said fondly. "Our in-house moral compass. We'll be more careful in the future about who we accuse. Is that enough? Can we get back to our lobsters now?"

Jessie pulled away and didn't answer. She looked around at her family and saw how they didn't have a clue what she meant about Aaron. The injury to Terri was lost on them. They had judged her guilty and were ready to move on.

"Well, what shall we do tomorrow?" her father was already saying, reaching for the coleslaw.

"Go to the beach!" Jonathan shouted.

"Go shopping," Julia said.

"A game of tennis?" their mother suggested.

In the end it rained and they all went to the movies.

*   *   *

The house was half packed for departure when word came
about Terri Carr.

Two full days of preparation were always necessary to
dislodge the Kettels once they'd settled into a place. That
summer, due to the length of their vacation, there had been
more settling than usual. Clothing, shoes, towels, and mag-
azines had migrated into unimaginable corners and parts of
the yard. Paperbacks, hats, sunscreen, dark glasses, and insu-
lated water flasks had escaped under couches and beds. The
Monopoly game and a number of puzzles had detonated into
crannies upstairs and down, along with Julia's endless bottles
of nail polish, which turned up everywhere, often capless,
fallen over or glued to the floor.

"I have never seen so much junk!" their father exclaimed.
"How did this family manage to accumulate such a mass of
possessions in such a short time? We didn't arrive with all
this, did we?"

Their mother had had the foresight to purchase a box of
large black plastic trash bags. "Throw away whatever you
won't absolutely need in Pittsburgh, or you won't fit in the
car," she advised her children. "That pile of flip-flops, for
instance. We'll never wear them in the city."

"But they're brand new. You just bought them!" her husband protested.

The phone rang. Richard Kettel answered. After a brief
conversation he replaced the receiver slowly in its old-
fashioned cradle.

"That was the police. Terri ran away from the correctional
center last night."

"Oh no," Julia said, looking at Jessie.

"They're asking us to keep a watch out for her. She might try to come back here. Well, not here here. She might try to get back home."

"How did she get away?" Julia asked.

"I don't know. She was supposed to have a hearing before a judge this morning. She bolted."

Their mother, coming in from the kitchen, shook her head.

"So sad," she said. "One of those terrible situations. Where's Jonathan?"

Jessie looked around. "Somewhere outside, I guess. He was playing with his magnifying glass."

"Would you go find him, Julia?"

"Why me? I was just—"

"Please find him. Now!" Marilyn Kettel ordered. "I don't want him outside by himself if that girl comes around here."

"Mom!" Jessie said. "It's just Terri. She loves Jonathan. She's the one who's been giving him all his best bugs."

"She'll never make it back here on her own anyway," their father added, broom in hand. "The correctional center is miles away. What would she do, hitchhike?"

"She might," their mother said. "I wouldn't put it past her."

Julia went outside. They heard her calling, "Spider boy! Where are you? Time to come back to the nest."

Jonathan answered at once. "Over here! Look what I found. A red ant!"

Richard Kettel chuckled. "See? Nothing to worry about.

Come on, back to work. Jessie, will you start packing Jonathan's clothes into his duffel? He can wear the clothes he's in now tomorrow in the car. We'll have to leave at the crack of dawn to drop your mother at the airport."

"Oh, heavens, don't worry about me. I can call a cab."

"Sweetie, we are not made of money! It would cost an arm and a leg to get a cab all the way down here."

A wild flame of hope had leaped up in Jessie when she heard that Terri had escaped. Irrational and illogical as it was, she hoped they wouldn't catch her. She saw her on the highway with her thumb out, accosting the flow of traffic with a defiant eye. She saw her jogging along back roads, making friends with stray cats, her pockets stuffed with sandwiches and candy bars. She saw her throwing away those horrible green pajamas, putting on her dirty cutoffs, polishing her name charm between two fingers. She saw her living free, the way she'd wanted to on the raft.

The raft.

She saw her out there on it.

All the rest of that afternoon Jessie kept an eye on the pond. She folded Jonathan's shirts and shorts and put them in his bag. She took her own clothes from the shelves in the closet and divided them into neat piles on her bed, ready to pack. In the kitchen she helped her mother empty out the refrigerator and sponge it clean. If there was a squawk outside, or a flutter or a splash, her heart jumped and she ran to look. A dark spot appeared on the water far down the pond as she was taking in beach towels off the line. She stood and

stared, afraid to let it out of her sight. But after a few minutes the spot rose into the air, spread wings, and flew away.

After dinner that evening Jessie went for a walk by herself. She said she wanted to say good-bye to the pond.

"I'm just going down to my old raft landing," she told her
mother. "Call if you need me. I'll be close by."

She didn't stay close by. As the sun dipped low on the
horizon, casting fiery streaks of pink and fuchsia in all directions, she set out along the path around the shore. She half
expected to find Terri back at her camp, cooking hot dogs
over a fire, the raft bobbing along the bank.

"I've been waiting for you," Terri would say. "I got your
note. Now we'll always be in touch. Isn't it great out here?"

"Beautiful," Jessie would say.

"See, it's not so bad as you thought it would be," Terri
would tell her. "We could live out here if we had to."

But the camp was deserted and obviously unvisited in
recent days. Jessie sat down on the stone table. She listened
to the pond. Sometimes, amidst the croaks and flutters, came
a watery sound, as if someone was out there just beyond her
rim of vision, poling warily through the water. She'd catch her
breath and think the raft was about to appear. But then the
sound would fade. The reeds would rattle and . . . nothing.

Evening was well under way but the sky was still light
when a rush of wings came from above. She looked up to see
masses of birds churning through the air. They flew in fan-
tastic formations, wheeling and swerving, swelling out into
clouds and thinning down into straight lines, hundreds of

birds moving together in perfect synchrony. As she watched, Julia came quietly beside her and sat down.

"Mom was worried about you. Sorry."

"It's okay. Look."

"What are they?"

"Starlings," Jessie said. "Terri told me. They do this at the end of the summer to get ready to migrate. Terri called it their ballet."

"How do they turn all at once? There must be one that gives the signal, or how would they know?"

"I don't know."

After a pause and still looking up, Julia said: "Any sign of her?"

"No."

"I thought you might've come out to look for her."

"I sort of did. I'm not sure she'll come back here, though. They'll be waiting for her."

"At the beach this morning people were saying there's new evidence about the fire. Now the police think it was started by a cigarette, like someone was smoking in there."

"You mean, instead of lighter fluid?"

"I guess. Anyway, there's some doubt about Terri setting the fire."

"There was always some doubt," Jessie said. "Everybody ganged up on her."

"But you thought she did it too, didn't you? You told Mom about her fire wand."

"I know. I got scared."

"So was it really broken? Mom thinks you made that up because you felt sorry for Terri."

"It wasn't broken," Jessie said. "I found it later and threw it in the pond. Terri would've had it with her if she'd used it to set the fire, wouldn't she?"

"I don't think that was up to you to judge," Julia said.

"Well, I did! Someone had to believe in her."

"If Terri didn't set that fire, why did she run away?" Julia said. "She should've waited to get cleared in court."

"People like her don't get cleared. Not like us. She knows that better than anyone."

"Well, they'll catch her," Julia said. "Then she'll get charged with breaking out and end up back in the correctional center anyway. Terri should get her act together and start figuring this stuff out. She should look ahead and make plans for herself."

"She *is* making plans!" Jessie said. "She's made them. She's getting out!" Her eyes filled with angry tears. "And I hope she makes it. She said she would in the end, and I believe her. She's the kind of person who doesn't give up."

Julia reached her arm around her sister's shoulders. "Don't get so upset. Terri Carr is not your problem."

"Yes, she is!" Jessie burst out, shrugging Julia's arm away. "She's my problem because I've seen her life, how stuck she is. Oh, Julia, I was so mean to her! I wouldn't hang out with her. I wouldn't give her my cell phone number when she asked. I didn't want her to call me."

"Anyone can see why."

"Well, I went over there later and left it for her. On the raft."

"Your cell phone number? You did? You went to the Carrs' house?"

Jessie nodded. "Don't ever tell Mom."

"Was anyone there?" Julia asked.

"Yes, Mitch. But he didn't see me. I left Terri the note and came home. I had to let her know where I'd be."

Julia gazed at her sister with an exasperated expression that was also part something else; perhaps it was admiration.

"You are a good person," Julia announced at last. "And completely nuts. What if Terri calls you? She probably will, you know. What will you do?"

"I'll be on her side," Jessie said. "Whatever she needs, I'll be there to help."

"You wouldn't have to," her sister said. "Nobody would know if you didn't. Nobody would even care."

"I know," Jessie answered, "and that's exactly why I'd do it."

Julia sighed. "You are so impossible. I can never tell what you're going to do next." Her arm went around Jessie's shoulders again, but in such an uncritical way that Jessie leaned closer to her.

They were silent for a long while after this. The surface of the pond turned a luminous pewter color, then dark blue, then black. Overhead, stars came out so distinctly that when the girls looked up, they were able to see the age-old designs they'd been taught as children.

"Look, the Big Dipper!"

"And the Little Dipper, I never can find that usually."

"There's the North Star!"

"There's Cassiopeia."

"Are those little ones the Pleiades?"

"At camp we called them the Seven Sisters."

"There's Andromeda!"

Somehow all this made it possible for Jessie to ask, "What happened with you and Ripley Schute?"

"He left. He had orientation or whatever. The freshmen go early to get to know the campus and see their dorms."

"So he didn't say good-bye?"

"No time," Julia said, a little too casually.

"I'm sorry I said that stuff about him. It's probably not even true. I just thought I'd pass it along."

"No, it's true," Julia said. "I asked around and got the real story. I pity the poor girl who gets invited to be his date at Princeton."

"He sounds terrible."

"Not terrible, just irresponsible. Immature. After a while you get to know who is and who isn't."

"I guess you figured him out."

"I did. So don't go saying those things to Mom. I know what I'm doing, okay?"

Jessie said okay. When another minute had passed, she leaned closer to Julia and said, "Listen, what's that noise? I keep hearing it."

"Sounds like someone swimming, or paddling in the water."

"It comes and goes. I hear it and then it fades away."

"Maybe someone's out there. What's that story, the one about the drowned boys?"

"The Peckham boys. They got caught in quicksand. There was a lot of it around in the old days, I guess. The pond was named for it."

"Sh-sh-sh." Julia hushed her. "There it is again."

They listened together. As they did, the sound rose and seemed to move nearer. Then, slowly, it diminished and was absorbed into the wallow and splash of the pond, into its shrieks and croaks and unidentifiable whispers. It was impossible for Jessie to determine whether this sound was something apart and distinct from all the others, or whether the wind was blowing at a different angle, bringing to her ears a new way of hearing a noise that had always been there.

TWENTY-FIVE

T wilight" is the word her mother used for this sweet
time of the day. Henrietta Cutting, ghosting downhill toward the pond, her feet barely touching the
ground, can still hear the way her mother said it: slow, the
vowels drawn out and flattened. "Ta-wahh-lahht." Amazing
after all these years how her voice remains in Henrietta's ear.
She's carried it with her like a song you learn when you're
young and can never forget no matter what has happened to
you or where you've ended up.

Henrietta has escaped from the house again. This time
there will be no calling her back. The girl with the dark hair,
the pond girl, is waiting on the raft below. She has come to
take Henrietta for a ride. Perhaps she'll let her handle the
raft pole this time. Henrietta's hands itch to hold it again, to
feel in charge of the how and the where of her going.

Somewhere in the grand house above her, Sally Parks is
taking a well-deserved snooze. The week's activities have
exhausted them both, starting with Henrietta's confusing
report to the policemen about the three men in gray coats.

Several more interviews were necessary before that story was assigned to its correct place in time. About events back then, more than seventy years ago, Henrietta's memory was so clear that Sally Parks had looked at her with new respect. The old woman named names, gave dates, showed a young reporter from the *Providence Evening News* the very dressing table she'd hidden under. It was still there in her mother's room, where nothing had changed in all those years.

"My father, George C. Cutting, owned your paper," Henrietta told him.

"This newspaper?" the young reporter asked.

"Yes."

"Mrs. Cutting—"

"Miss Cutting," Henrietta interrupted. "I never married. And never will." She looked down sadly at her hands.

What an interesting figure she was. So misunderstood. So tormented by life. Photographers from the newspaper arrived to take her photo. But since she refused to come downstairs, they had to content themselves with a shot of Sally Parks, in full form, standing on the veranda. (Sally was thrilled!)

State officials began a new investigation of the Cutting murders. Once again the terrible event became front-page news. Three mobsters were implicated, though not one of them was still alive. The old photo of Henrietta as a girl was located in the newspaper archives and printed again. It was the one that showed her with what everyone thought was a fishing pole over her shoulder.

"So you were never once asked about the murders?"

Sergeant Smith returned to inquire. His companion now was an FBI agent. "How is that possible?"

"I was a child." Henrietta shrugged. "No one cared to really listen. The police were so sure they had the right man."

"But you were there. You saw it happen. You could've spoken for Eddie Carr."

"I tried," Henrietta said. "Over many years. Eddie's dead now, you know."

"We know. We checked."

"A life ruined," Henrietta said. "More than one," she added, with a look at her visitors.

Under these circumstances the investigation of the fire in the garage took a backseat. Henrietta continued to support the pond girl. ("Why are you holding her? Let her come home. She was nowhere near my landing!") The police were still not convinced, but since no further evidence against the girl could be found, they decided (for the time being) to let her go. Terri Carr was on the brink of being released from the Canville Correctional Center when she escaped. She slipped out an unguarded bathroom window and vanished into the night.

She disappeared.

The next afternoon Henrietta received a phone call from the police asking her to watch out for Terri—the same warning Jessie's father received as the Kettels packed to leave. Sally Parks, standing by the old woman, saw her lurch up from her chair. The telephone dropped from her hand.

"Miss Cutting, what's wrong? You're pale as a radish."

"She's coming," Henrietta breathed.

"What?"

"She'll be here soon! She's coming back."

"Please. Henrietta. Sit down. You don't look well. Whatever it is, I'm sure this can't be good for your heart."

Back and forth from the kitchen Sally flew, with milk, cranberry juice, cookies, sandwiches, a special medication for moments of overexcitement. The old lady would not be quieted. She was "in a wild state." This was how Sally would describe it later.

That was this afternoon. Now it is twilight and Henrietta has come out of her chair by the window. She was sitting there, watching the pond, and now she has left it and is floating downhill on the lightest of feet. She sees the raft approaching the landing on her shore. The pond girl is on it, waving. They will meet again at last!

"I told them you were not responsible," Henrietta will say when they are together. "I saw you on the raft. I knew you weren't to blame for the fire."

"Thank you," the girl will say. "Where can I take you on this beautiful evening?"

"I would like to go across to visit the gray foxes," Henrietta tells her, for suddenly, with no effort at all, the future is the present and she has arrived at the shore. The raft is ready. The girl is helping her aboard.

"We could live over there if you like," the girl says, pushing off with the pole.

"I would like that very much," Henrietta replies.

Acknowledgments

I would like to thank my editor, Emma Ledbetter, whose insight into and enthusiasm for this novel made all the difference. I'm also grateful to my agent and colleague, Gina Maccoby, for her unwavering faith in me over many years.